STONEWALL INN EDITIONS

Keith Kahla, General Editor

12.95

6.50

F

D0376879

GLOVE PUPPET

GLOVE PUPPET

NEAL DRENNAN

ST. MARTIN'S PRESS ❧ NEW YORK

GLOVE PUPPET. Copyright © 1998 by Neal Drinnan. All rights reserved.
Printed in the United States of America. No part of this book may be
used or reproduced in any manner whatsoever without written permis-
sion except in the case of brief quotations embodied in critical articles or
reviews. For information, address St. Martin's Press, 175 Fifth Avenue,
New York, N.Y. 10010.

Library of Congress Cataloging-in-Publication Data

Drinnan, Neal, 1964–
    Glove puppet / Neal Drinnan.
        p. cm.
    ISBN 0-312-19271-1 (hc)
    ISBN 0-312-24444-4 (pbk)
    I. Title.
PR9619.3.D78G58   1998
823—dc21   98-28866
                                                                 CIP

First published in Australia by Penguin Books Australia Ltd.

First Stonewall Inn Edition: October 1999

            10 9 8 7 6 5 4 3 2 1

FOR TIM

Acknowledgements

I would like to acknowledge Bryony Cosgrove, Helen Pace, James Bradley, Lyn Amy, David Nair, Michael West, Kirk Drinnan and David Wills for all their support and encouragement

I learned there are troubles
Of more than one kind.
Some come from ahead
And some come from behind.

But I've bought a big bat
I'm ready, you see
Now my troubles are going
To have trouble with *me!*

from **I Had Trouble in Getting to Solla Sellew**
DR SEUSS

GLOVE PUPPET

PROLOGUE

Victoria Station yawned like a cavernous mouth, signalling the end of our journey. My first journey and my mother's last.

Mum was shivering and edgy, scared to disembark. I was jumping in and out, back and forth, as if to show her it was no big deal – train, platform, train, platform. I was mocking her indecision, limbre and lithely.

'Fucken' knock it off Johnny or I'll belt ya . . .'

Her voice caught in her throat, like she was going to be sick.

The man who'd said he was a doctor caught our eye as he stepped from another carriage. We both watched him slink out through one of the exits. I with relief, Mum with poisoned despair. His dirty vinyl bag full of nasty tricks hung awkwardly across his shoulder, making of him a grotesquely degenerate schoolboy. His beady little eyes were darting all over the joint, but he never looked at us again. He had the cowering manner of a guilty dog who'd just snaffled up a dirt-poor family's supper. If I'd been big enough, I'd have beaten him with a stick, a good, thick nursery rhyme faggot barbed with a crooked rusty nail. The train doors finished their clatter of opening and slamming. I was impatient, 'C'mon Ma, let's go.'

It was just us now, frail and forlorn on a dim platform in a vast grey space. A posh, recorded voice offered monotonous information about trains, trains going places that meant nothing to us. A chubby guard, keen to be knocking off for the night, passed by, cursing the sloppy mess from a pie he'd just spilled down his front. 'All bloody gravy, not an ounce of meat,' he muttered.

I fancied some of that pie, meat or gravy, but Mum, she couldn't look at it. She was feeling sick. Sometimes it was like that after she'd had her needle. We trudged across the deserted platform to a dingy alcove where she slid onto the grotty wooden bench, and groaned with relief as she weighed into its cold, hard comfort. 'Mum needs a rest, Love – 'ere's a pound, go get yourself a pie.'

There was no one around except for a man in another alcove nearby. He was huddled into his coat reading the paper, a single suitcase between his legs. When he noticed I was staring as I dawdled past he said, 'Hello.'

I was watching him because he looked like the host on a nightly game show Mum used to watch. I think she was keen on that man on TV. She'd laugh and say, ''Ere Johnny, you's al'ays on about wantin' to know who ya father is, well it's 'im, 'im on telly.' I wondered if this man was the same one. I'd never seen anyone off the telly before.

'Are you on the telly?' I asked.

He sort of cocked his head and smiled in a funny way.

'I've been on the telly, if that's what you mean.'

'Oh, me Mum likes you'n'all.'

He looked over at Mum, who'd slid sideways and was sleeping.

'Is your Mum alright?'

'She's a bit sick, s'all.'

'Perhaps we ought to get her some help. Is she very sick?'

'She's awright, she jus' gets sick wi' someat in 'er stomach 'at's all.'

He didn't seem convinced. I wandered off in search of my pie.

I left the platform and went into the vast entrance hall, gasping at its size. The queen would live somewhere like this, I thought. Most of the shops were closed. I passed an old bag lady who was talking to herself, a slumped, sleeping man who'd wet his trousers and another man cuddling an ancient dog with hardly any fur. I asked the lady at a kiosk for a pie. She gave it to me while scanning the concourse for an adult I might be attached to.

'Love, where's your Mum or Dad?'

'Oh, me Dad's out there.' I gestured towards the platforms. ''E's on the telly me Dad is.'

'Well now there's a thing,' she said, reassured by the knowledge of guardians unseen.

I stood, looking around, eating my lukewarm pie, then, having fingered out the cold part with a dirty splat onto the

3

tiled floor, I headed back to Mum, pastry crust and change in hand.

I wandered slowly past the handsome man again, flaunting my pie crust as if it were worthy of envy, a priceless coronet plucked and flaunted from our family jewels. I squeezed the coins in my other hand, hoping Mum would forget about the change. I was hoping maybe he'd talk to me some more.

'Was that a nice pie?'

'Nah, it was bleedin' cold.'

'Are you sure your Mum's okay?'

'I told ja, she's jus' a bit sick.'

I headed back to Mum, annoyed by all these questions. I remembered what she'd said back home about police, social workers and the like: 'World's full of nosy bloody Parkers.' I looked at the man again. No one understood about when she got sick; soon she'd be up wanting a cup of tea. I looked in my palm and closed it again. I didn't know how much a cup would cost but it didn't look like enough in there to buy her one, not enough for chips or anything.

I finished the pie and sat awhile watching Mum. She looked like a doll, no colour in her face except the make-up she was wearing. She was sweating and cold. Since I'd been away she'd vomited onto the ground. I was very tired by then, so I curled myself near her, my back against the cold drafts, my head near the vague warmth of her lap. I didn't like our chances in London so far.

'What's that you got, Johnny?' It was a hot day, warmer than the warmest day on Brighton Beach, and Mum was all better. She had on her dressing-gown, the silky summer one with big flowers on it. She was smiling and squinting in the sun's glare. 'It's a flower Mum, a big white 'n' yellow flower, smells nice 'n' all.' I went to give it to her but she shook her head. 'You keep it Love, there's plen'y 'ere.' I looked around and she was right; flowers just like it were everywhere. 'You'll be awright ya hear?' She was going somewhere I couldn't follow. I looked deep into the flower and breathed its perfume. A warm smell, a clean smell.

I woke with a start; the TV man was lifting me in his arms. 'We've got to get your Mum to hospital. I've rung for an ambulance,' he said.

Mum was cold. I tried to grab her leg as he lifted me but it was limp. As he drew me to him I smelt that same warm, clean smell.

Real things, by then, had taken on a dreamlike quality. Ambulance men came and a stretcher was wheeled in while a couple of bleary-eyed hobos and the crazy bag lady I'd spotted out on the concourse had begun to gather for what promised to be a show. The bag lady began to shout. 'It's drugs what does it to 'em, I've seen more 'n' one go that way with the drugs.'

She sidled up to us like some pantomime dame, her bottle of sherry ready to fall from her open bag, her vile breath silencing me in the man's arms.

''Ere, don't you let your littl'un look at that, 's not right at his age, all them tarts come to same end with drugs nowadays, not like in the war.'

His brow furrowed and he whispered something to me, something that kept me quiet, about getting out of there safely, about being saved and about a game.

'Just imagine we're on a bridge miles above a cold and stormy sea.'

I thought of Brighton Beach in the dead of winter and shivered.

'I am the bridge, my arms are the supports and when I put you down again you'll know we're safe, so keep quiet and I'll get you across.'

I wasn't scared. In some way the bridge seemed to make sense. I knew something very bad had happened but I didn't move. There was magical strength in those arms, a benevolence in his eyes that hypnotised me, inspired hope somehow. Perhaps he really was my father; he'd already paid me more attention than the thousand other men who might have been my dad. I half wanted to yell out to Mum, but I think I knew she was dead. The muscly arms formed a parapet, a real protection from all that strife, from all those waiting freaks, which I would have been forced to join had he not picked me up.

An ambulance attendant came over and asked the man if he knew Mum.

The bag lady interrupted, 'I was just saying to the nice gent'y'man he shouldn't let his boy see that, them tarts fillin' 'emselves wi' drugs, I 'spect you've seen it all before, but 's not for kids to be seeing.' She was coming at me, trying to touch my face. The man kept turning me so I wouldn't have to endure her inquisitive prods.

'No,' he said calmly in answer to the ambulance attendant. As he did so the bag lady sent her sherry bottle smashing to the ground. 'We were on our way to the tube when I noticed the state she was in.' The man gestured towards Mum, not to the bag lady, who was now on her knees assessing the shattered bottle.

I was distracted by the woman, who had managed to salvage a small quantity of sherry in the jagged remains of the bottle and was trying to work out which angle was safest to drink it from without cutting her lips.

The man was holding my bag, a plastic one from Sainsburys with spare clothes and a toy lorry in it. It suddenly dawned on me that 'we' meant him and me. I asked whether on the bridge I was safe from witches. He told me I was. I asked if the woman was a witch. 'I fear so, I fear so very much.' The bag lady eyed me suspiciously and I decided I'd stay on the bridge a while longer. I felt if he dropped me, I would fall into a coldness and blackness from which I could never return.

The ambulance attendant seemed relieved this was a straight pick-up. No lifesaving required; just midnight in the meat wagon, another dead junkie. 'All aboard – let's move 'er out.' They hauled my Mum onto a stretcher. I watched, silently, and wondered who this man was and what he might do to me. Would he be like the man in the black anorak who gave the other boys on the estate a whole pound one day? He'd gotten cross when they wriggled. What had made them wriggle, I wondered, and was it worth a pound? This man seemed different. I might like him, and as the moment for me to yell out came and went I thought about myself without a mother. There was no reason to think I was any better off with those ambulance attendants than I was with this nice-smelling man. Besides, I knew everyone had to wriggle somewhere along the line if they wanted to survive. Mum taught me that much.

It wasn't until after they'd loaded her onto the trolley, strapped her onto a stretcher, pulled the sheet over her and wheeled her off into the night that my sobbing began. The man carried his tearful child and his suitcase down into the tiled, eerie silence of the London underground. I felt so tired and weak a breeze could have carried me off. Crying never did much good with Mum – why should he have been fussed by it any more than her?

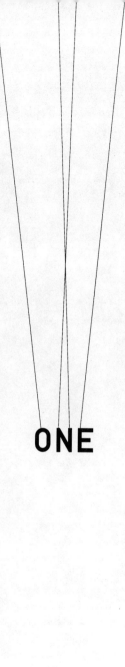

ONE

L O S T
B O Y

I don't even try wishing for things to be the way they used to be. That's the first rule of growing up. All that wishing shit I left behind. But some residues just won't go away. I still wake up in a sweat; I am jolted from my subconscious by the impact of colliding cars. I am in the car, but am I the driver? I never know.

Brigitte helps me with my dreams. She tells me it will emerge one day and when it does, it will be a breakthrough. 'Was I driving? Was I driving?' I chant to myself as I lie clutching the damp French knot of sheets that have gathered beneath me. Cars cruise past my window, the beams from their headlights casting strange shadows and rare illuminations on my peeling walls. I shudder, cringing like a child afraid of the dark, a boy who might still need Mum or Dad to protect him from the bogeyman. But the bogeyman has already come for them, delivered them to their own private darknesses, and I lie shivering silently, waiting for my turn.

My heart thunders inside me like a galloping horse on hard, dusty turf. I feel as though I am about to have a heart attack. Other times it's a kind of swoon I feel, waking out of something heavenly, something deliriously pleasurable and desperately erotic. Something perfect yet tainted by an underlying and ever-attendant menace. I sense that something very bad would come of my dream had I not woken.

'You can't have a heart attack at 20,' I tell myself. I am young, strong, and my life is nowhere near over yet. I remember what Brigitte said: 'Go back into the dreams, take them all on, fight them, fuck them, do whatever they want if it's the same as what you want, but learn in your dreams that the terms are yours. Your dreams are your freedom and you've every right to demand your freedom.'

The drugs don't help, especially acid, K, MDA and ecstasy. Even the mind-deadening tranquillisers I take to counter them have their dark side. It's not the same bedroom either, not as grand as the one in Paddington with its billowing white curtains, polished boards and huge bed in the centre of the room. How sturdy a vessel that bed proved on balmy summer nights; it sighed, it grunted while we moaned or wept. It seemed to float on the ether of the night. Our magic carpet over Sydney.

The city in all its glittering splendour pulsed outside the full-length sash windows, breathing and gasping in time with its children. Flesh dollies, only minutes away, danced on balconies just like ours, swinging their hips like trashy neon advertisements for warm, moist flesh pockets. Who will buy? Who will buy? How slick, how tempting is sex without love. And all about us, penis pushers, drug pedlars and party people searched for something cold to drink, something hot to fuck. Yet sin wasn't what I yearned for from the city's dark-wall streets or its hole-in-the-wall sleaze clubs. Sin was as vague a notion as I could ever have.

I was the answered prayer, the orphaned child, the victim. I was the bottled rage of the primly dressed woman who wants to have her say on *Oprah*. I was the one we would all love and take in to our hearts and homes if only we could get him out of the telly, out of the institution, out of the abusive family.

Strange how the drugs make me feel – as though I can conjure him up again, as if my imagination can turn air into matter, emptiness into rapture, nervousness into security. Other times they do the opposite, making the past come back.

You probably want to know what Glove Puppet means and who the fuck I am. Well no one calls me that any more, or not to my face. You probably wonder why I'm writing a biography at the age of 20. I'm not famous, I'm not a supermodel, nor am I a former child star from a popular TV series. But I was famous three years ago. That's why I have to write about what happened. Everyone read the papers, they all had opinions, but there's a lot of stuff that no one knows.

Brigitte reckons I should write everything down, including my dreams. Maybe she's right and maybe if I could get my shit together I could sell the real story about what happened to some magazine; maybe the very same ones that made our lives hell. 'Think of writing as a form of exorcism,' Brigitte says. I haven't got too much to lose and I'd love to lift 25,000 dollars out of the coffers of some of those magazines. I've heard that's how much they'd pay me for a story like mine. Maybe even more.

I don't stay in all the time. I prefer the night for going out. Sometimes with my posse, which seems to change from month to month, or sometimes just on my own. It only takes me five minutes to get to Oxford Street, and these days I command a little bit of respect even if I'm still whispered about. Of course people are as nice as pie if they want something from you – an E, some speed or a trip. I don't handle the H one though – not after what happened to my Mum – and even the others I just dabble in a little bit, you know, for friends or acquaintances. Trouble is, once people get stuff from you, they never leave you alone. You've got to be careful too; there is some serious trash in this town and nobody is particularly discreet. Most of these fucking 18-year-olds are just trying to make the scene. They'll talk about having you as their dealer as quickly as they'll say Anaesthezïa from Dizztopia is their hairdresser.

Things have been pretty scary lately. This guy – and I'm not naming names – he went to RENTBaa on one of their big party nights, and he was selling trips to a whole lot of people who were already really shit-faced. Well, he thought it would be a bit of a lark to cut up those cardboard roach mats which are profoundly toxic and sell them as trips, cheap trips, 10 bucks each. That price alone would have set alarms ringing

14

with me but some of the punters in those clubs are total airheads; they would buy anything just to be cool and wasted. The upshot of that particular night of enterprise was that the only trip people got was to St Vincent's Hospital. There were eight casualties. These things tasted so bad that no one would have sucked them for any length of time no matter how out of it they were.

Estelle (the girl from the moon) was around here the next day with her space cadet girlfriend, *Marie Claire* (she named herself after the magazine), and they reckoned one chick died from them. She was found in the lane round the back, but there are other rumours that she was murdered. Estelle says the reason she died from it was because she stuck the roach mat up her arse like a suppository. According to *Marie Claire*, any person tasteless enough to carry a Chanel handbag down Oxford Street is asking for trouble.

I look at her multiple piercings, her pink leatherette hot pants and her torn 70s lime green halter-neck held together with nappy pins and wonder where the true definition of taste resides. 'Those suburban slags come in here of a Saturday night, all of them thinking their cunts are sweet enough to turn those gay boys straight. Next Mardi Gras they should just get a whole train of hoppers packed full of dead slags and all those straight boys can jump 'em as they trundle past.'

There was a picture in the *Telegraph* of the hopper they found this girl in but all you could see in the grainy photo was a pathetic patent leather platform shoe and the Chanel handbag. I'm no detective but you don't usually find the Chanel-handbag-brigade sticking drugs up their arses. Her

15

Mum's doing a story in *Who* next week. It'll be the usual *'She was just out for a night with her girlfriends, they never usually drink that much and they certainly don't take drugs.'* She'll probably turn out to be a nurse or some other icon of goodness and hope.

The way I see it, if you were dying from poisoning, why would you throw yourself in a hopper down a lane? I reckon someone done her in. I did ring the police – anonymously – to say who I thought sold those trips. He's totally out there, that guy. If he knew I'd told, he'd kill me for sure.

The problem with all these murders is no one ever finds out the truth. The papers run all these stories about people who are dumped on the Cahill Expressway or promising models who disappear from service stations. The media loves freshly damaged or dead meat. They love deciding posthumously that some two-bit waif-cum-model was going to be the next Elle Macpherson or Linda Evangelista, but it's no use getting hooked on the stories because they never get followed up. Drug-related, prostitution-related, thrill kill or just good ol' kiss the girls and make them die. You never find out.

I should concentrate on the real source of my troubles. How things turned very bad for me and nightmarish for my Dad. If it's all going to come out I have to go back to where it started – where I started.

Mum and I lived somewhere near Brighton – Brighton in England. She was a hard-working whore with five or six tattoos and blonde hair, though I'm sure it wasn't naturally blonde.

We lived in a three-room council flat, and somehow she avoided the social workers who would have taken me away if they'd known what went on. Mum was 16 when she had me. I had no father, or perhaps I had a thousand – depends how you view it. Whatever the case, I doubt she could have told you who he was any more than I can. She was on the pension, but that wasn't enough, not for the smack as well.

Mum wasn't your model parent; my earliest memories were of her lying on the bed trying to zip up her jeans with a coat-hanger then clomping around in ferociously high platform shoes. Her tits always seemed as if they were just about to fall out of her top, and on her left breast she had a tat of a heart being carried off by a bird. I loved that tattoo, perhaps in my subconscious it related to breastfeeding; as I sucked, the breast bobbed, the bird seemed to fly. Feeding and movement. It seemed strange that she'd go to such trouble to get those jeans on when they were always being taken off, but I suppose that was the fashion for tarts then and there was no mistaking Mum for anything else.

We had a vague routine of events each day – I remember the hollow clomp of those vinyl shoes along the balcony of our tenement and down our road. I guess because of the smack Mum didn't eat much herself, so in the shop she just bought things for me: cheesesticks, crisps, little plastic containers of jelly or mousse, baby food (even though I was far too old for it), chocolate, Bakewell tarts, sweets with cheap plastic toys attached. Anything bright or trippy that caught her eye. When we got home from the shops I would play with all the food and coloured toys on the kitchen floor. If Mum hadn't met someone down the street who wanted to come back and fuck her then there would probably be someone who just turned up at the door. The winter used to be busier than the summer. Strange, you'd think it'd be the other way around. I remember warm days down on the pier, going on the big candy-coloured slippery dip.

I played on the dirty lino floor by the radiator, breaking or chewing off the plastic wheels on the sherbet train, trying to get the last of the processed cheese out of the cheesestick wrapper. Each day's stuff piled up. I hated any of yesterday's things and the day before's I loathed even more. I watched the telly on the kitchen table while Mum was shagged senseless in the next room or pumped full of smack. Sometimes she would get knocked around a bit but you don't feel it so much on smack, or so they tell me. Some days, four or five of them would come through, so I couldn't tell which one had given her the bruise. Besides, she wore so much mascara and eyeliner that by the end of the day she looked like she had black eyes anyway.

To be fair to her she must have loved me in her own way. She kissed me and played with me between 'clients', but she treated me more like a dream she was having than a child. She used to love Stevie Nicks; sometimes when she got quite out of it she'd play 'Rhiannon' on this old cassette player we had. She'd dance about in her dressing-gown like Kate Bush, a scarf draped, shawl-like, around her and platform boots like the ones Stevie wore. She would pretend to be that gipsy-hearted witch. Mum probably dreamt of having witches' powers, of having any power at all. I would clap when she finally curled, foetus-like, on the floor, the tape warbling to an end.

The sound of shagging was the muzak of my childhood. I made a close study of those sounds, time and movement, good and bad. Bad was when they wanted things Mum wouldn't give them, when she yelled at them, told them to 'sod off'. Good was when she stayed 'in character' for the whole performance, when their demands were simple, when she was compliant. I would think about the different amount of time it took each of them to go to the toilet in Mum. Often I ate a crisp for each grunt made by the man. Once I was doing just this when the man grunting, farted. Did I eat a crisp for this sound also? And if I did would I fall out of step with the grunts which were continuing, quite oblivious to the fart?

Sometimes Mum left the door ajar. I could peek in if I wanted but I didn't always like looking – it was often the hairy arse of some bloke pointing at me, pounding madly into her. I didn't like the hairy ones, nor the fat ones, but some were slim and smooth. There was something I yearned for from those; perhaps it was envy that flickered like a snake's tongue in my heart as Mum danced to a wild beat I could only imagine, a rhythm both exciting and repellent.

There were occasions when the movements varied. Some liked to get slightly different thrusting angles, perhaps to favour one part of their cock or maybe they wanted to try positions with Mum that they weren't allowed with their girlfriends or their wives or the retarded lady in the next Close who did it for free while her own mother was at Bingo. On her good days Mum moaned a bit as if she liked it. Maybe she did. Other times she'd just be quiet, preferring to let them make all the noise. I peered in, crisps or cheesestick in hand and took it all in, the endless parade of arses, the smell of semen and body odour – you'd think it would put you off sex, wouldn't you?

I went to school, in the end. I was 6 when I started; I should have gone the previous year but it must have slipped past Mum until a social worker came and chided her for not sending me. Once I was at school she tried to do most of her work during the day but there were always some who preferred the evening.

I would get fish and chips for supper, or sometimes Mum cooked me egg and bacon with toast. I don't think she knew what a vegetable was. On her days of relative clarity we had oranges and apples from the greengrocer, but Mum preferred never to go anywhere but the corner shop. I walked to school each day and probably got the best food I'd ever had as school dinners.

Around the tenements after school I mucked about with urchins like myself; grubby, dough-faced boys raised on potatoes and lard or sharp-faced, street-smart kids used to dodging their father's drunken backhands. The sea, at least, was not far away. There was a playground down there where a man in a black anorak sometimes went. He would give us 20 pence, or more, if we showed him our doodles. We would go to that park, hoping he'd be there so we could buy some sweets or a big greasy mess of chips with the doodle money. We'd huddle around the broken swings, squabbling like seagulls over our steaming hot reward. Smelling and eating chips was always a treat. Sitting huddled on the ground, clenching my bottom, which was often a little hot and sore from Anorak Man's meddling inquisitiveness. Each boy hungry and quiet, keeping his fingers warm in the oily newspaper as our burning breath sent silent, vaporous SOS rings up into a freezing, colourless sky.

After the chips we wandered around, breaking the things we were strong enough to break, trying to break the things we weren't. We terrorised old ladies at the bus stop who, at first, would try to be sweet to us but who quickly realised we were not the type of children worth being sweet to. The other kids usually got called in for their supper, but Mum wasn't a 'come on Love, your supper's on the table' sort of Mum, nor was she a 'What time do you call this?' sort of Mum when I came in at 8 or 9 of an evening.

In the winter it seemed to be dark all the time. Kids stayed in more and I didn't get invited around to other kids' flats. 'Our Ma says you can't come to our house, she says you're common and you i'nt got a proper Dad or nuffink and your Mum's bad.' Well the other families were hardly what you'd call blue bloods, scarcely qualifying as working class most of them because social security isn't work afterall. Once the girls heard the taunts about Mum and me at school, their skipping ropes quickly whipped rumours into a song. A song Mum refused to ever hear. A song I still remember.

Knock knock who's at the door
dirty Johnny Smith whose Mum's a whore
Knock knock what's that sound
she's even dirtier for five pound
Knock knock make that ten
she'll drop her knickers down and do it all again

I knew that all those groans from the other room were the source of that badness. I never had anyone to our flat, either. Even then I was ashamed of the mess in our place, and the smell. Heroin leaves a sweet smell on the skin of the user.

A couple of times blokes moved in for a while but moved out just as quickly. They were all junkies and each one realised, pretty fast, that Mum's 'relative prosperity' came from between her legs; that unless they went out to work she would have to keep doing what she was doing to keep the smack coming in and to keep me in fish and chips.

They argued about smack; about whose turn it was to go to the shop, whose turn to score, who was going to 'cook up'. They lived on Coca-Cola and cups of tea, occasionally having some chocolate or chips while I ate baby food out of crusty plastic bowls with one of many blackened spoons.

When we got new neighbours next door – Mum called the woman a nosy bloody Parker – that must have been the beginning of the end. One night the bloke who came around was pretty drunk. The door was ajar and I looked in because of the commotion. This bloke was laying into Mum good and proper. She had been giving him oral, which cost 10 pounds extra (I had heard these things negotiated). His dick was limp; I suspect he was too pissed to get it up, either that or he was impotent anyway. He was yelling, 'You really are a filfy old slapper injcha, you's just a filfy whore what's more full o'drugs van full o' cock.' He hit her a couple of times across the face and I ran in screaming. She turned on him, shrieking like a banshee, 'You can't even get'cha useless fuckin' prick up ya' pratt, fuck off outa here why don'cha.' And amidst my screams and hers he did.

The nosy Parker from next door came and got in on the act: 'Don't think I don't know what sort o' discustin' business goes on in here you filthy tart, it's nowt more than a knock-up shop and I'm reporting you to the DSS. You're not fit to bring up a little'un in that pigsty and I can't be doing with all this noise not with the baby asleep ——'

Mum went at her with a broom (it was the only time I ever saw her pick it up). It was a terrible fight, and someone must have phoned the police. I guess Mum tried to think fast. She threw stuff into a bag, told me to put clothes on over my pyjamas and said we had to go. We went to the station and got on a late train to London. Perhaps things would be different there. Perhaps the streets were paved with gold, or at least paved with smack.

Mum started to sweat and shiver on the train. She needed her medicine. A vile-looking bloke sitting near us started watching her and finally came over.

'You awright Love?' He was looking at the developing bruise under her left eye.

'Yeah, me old man and I just had a bit of a fallin' out s'all.'

'Sure you did Love, and what sort a' bloke'd knock a lovely piece o' skirt like you around?' Mum sort of smiled, but even I could see that 'lovely piece of skirt' was not an apt description. I also knew that the smile was not the modest smile of a grateful lady. Mum was desperate and anything could happen on this trip to London. No Buckingham Palace or changing of the guard would this Johnny see.

''Ere, Love, I reckon I got a bit o' someat you might fancy.' He fished around in a dirty old vinyl airline bag and pulled out a white plastic sachet.

Her eyes lit up a little. 'What you want for that, then?'

'Nuffink too demandin.' Just a little bit of 'vem comforts what your old man won't be gettin' tonight.'

He looked at me and smiled. 'Don't you worry young lad, I'm a doctor and I wanna get your lovely Mum all nice and well again.'

I had seen some nasty-looking doctors down at the clinic where Mum went intermittently, but never had they looked as wretched as this one. Greasy hair, yellow teeth. He was Fagin on drugs.

Mum needed her medicine, however, and whether it was smack, icing sugar, rat poison or dishwasher powder she was going into the toilet on that train to earn it. I waited outside. We were only 15 minutes from London but I had seen her earn money in much less than 15 minutes.

He came out first, tucking in his shirt. He looked sheepishly at me then slunk off down the other end of the train. Mum came out holding her arm. She was in pain, and there was blood on her jumper. She was still shaking a little and something seemed wrong, by wrong I mean more than usually wrong – wrong, for me, was right.

CURE

I was abducted. Adopted. The man at the station was the most handsome man I'd ever seen. If he had said he was a doctor I might have believed him. He wore a long, dark coat. I suspected him of being magical in some way. He carried me down to the tube station at Victoria and sat with me. He talked quietly about how we were safe from the witch, how my Mum was safe from everything and how there was still a way to go before we were completely safe. He waited patiently until my sobbing had ceased. Then he began talking in that same voice that had so mesmerised me before.

'Do you have a Dad anywhere?'

I shook my head. He sounded like one of the posh people on the telly.

'Do you know your Dad's name?'

'I just told ya I 'int got a Dad.'

'Perhaps you'd like to have one,' he said.

I started to cry again. Mum was, after all, the only person in the world I could call family. Hers was the only care I'd experienced and however dubious that care had been it was the only thing I'd ever taken for granted.

'I better have someone or I'll get meself lost. If you is takin' me some'ere you better not do nuffink bad to me,' I said, mustering all the council estate bravado I could. He bit his bottom lip and his eyes took on a tearful shine. He put his hand on my head and pulled me towards him. I wrapped my arms around him and held on. I did the destitute child perfectly. The poignancy was not lost on my new benefactor. I think that was when I realised I would go with him. What else would I have done? I'd missed my chance at turning myself in to the vagaries of State benevolence. If I didn't go with him what would I do? Who or what would I get instead?

'I know how I could make you safe. I have a bit of a plan.' He took two booklets from his coat pocket. 'Passports,' he said, and looked at a picture in one of them. He looked at me, then at the passport again. He seemed to smile for a second, then he looked panicked for a bit, running his hand through his heavy dark fringe. He glanced about nervously; there was no one around. A cold gust of wind blasted out of the tunnel, reminding me of the coming winter. A wasted-looking punk was arguing with his heavily made-up girl-friend. They had a cassette player and were listening to The Cure; it echoed bleakly down the platform on that same chill November wind. Once the man was sure they weren't inter-ested in us, he began talking to me in a hushed, forthright and serious tone:

'If you want to have a Dad, someone to get you away from here safely, I could pretend it was me, but you'd have to do what I say. If I give you to the police they will take you to some home full of other children. Do you want to go there?'

I thought about a home full of other children, children even poorer than me and the girl at school who lived with another family and had to pretend it was hers because her own parents were dead or didn't want her or something. At least my Mum put up a fight when the welfare lady came around to our place every few months. 'Stupid fat cow,' Mum'd say after she'd been. 'Al'ays picken on us what 'aven't got blokes. *"What do ya' give 'im for 'is tea, are you seein' a fella at the moment?"* All bloody hoity-toity them welfare cows, they'd lock you up at Borstal Johnny if I let 'em 'ave their bloody way. Just cos I don't work at Little Chef like 'er downstairs. Well I do better 'n 'er. My boy's fed I'll 'ave ya know. 'E's better fed than some whats fathers spend every bloody penny they get on lager.' She declared these things as addendums to no one in particular and always after the lady had gone. She never got cross while the woman was visiting. I wondered what this man might have to offer; it was at least worth finding out.

'If you come with me, I could help you to make a happier new life and I will look after you very well. If you come with me now we will get on an aeroplane and live in Australia. It's a long journey and we'll have to play another game to get there, but we will get away from all this cold. I could take you to the welfare people but if you do want to come with me I have an aeroplane ticket for you, a special ticket for a boy your age. We can't help your Mummy anymore. It's very sad I know but you have to leave her behind. Wherever you go, God is looking after her now.'

I knew nothing of God; I had no concept of what sort of thing he/she/it was. But the aeroplane had already done it; to go on an aeroplane I would have done anything.

'Awright, jus' remember what I said before, you promise you won't do nuffink bad to me.'

He took my hand. 'I would never hurt you. I had a little boy your age who died just a couple of weeks ago. You look rather like him, you look the same age and if you really think there is no one else who would look after you or miss you, then we could pretend you were him, but you'll have to do as I say or we'll never get past all of the police.'

I had inherited my mother's distrust of the 'filth'. I already had a sense that authority in general was out to get Mum and me in one way or another. Suddenly the idea of such deception seemed like a very exciting idea, like one of those TV shows where the kids get away with all sorts of pranks. And I had my heart set on that aeroplane ride. I knew my choices were desperately limited. Somewhere beneath all the fear, exhaustion and grief, excitement stirred. I imagined telling all the boys on the estate about going on a plane. Not one of them had been on a plane. For me it was adventure on a grand scale. Poor Mum, her memory being traded in for a plane ticket as quickly as she might have traded me for a much needed hit.

He said I was to call him Dad and that he would call me Vas from then on.

'Vas?' I asked. 'What sor' o' name is 'at?'

He showed me 'my' British passport. 'It's short for Vaslav.' There was a photograph of a woman and a child in it – a mother and son passport. 'Posh git,' I said. I could not remember ever having possessed a bowtie like the boy in the photo, but I did look like him a bit. We both had longish hair. The passport was two years old, and kids grow and change quickly. I looked at 'Dad'. I said, 'Is he dead?' The man nodded sadly. I wanted to know how he had died. I only ever knew of one kid who died. He was a thin, pale kid who went home sick from school and never came back. Miss had come in one day and said that Mickey Macmasters had died from leukemia. I never even knew what the word meant. I asked if this 'Vas' boy had died of leukemia, and the man said no.

I didn't ask any more questions, I didn't want to jeopardise that plane ride. And even if I had to run away from this man when we got to Australia I couldn't see how it could be worse than where I was. If the boy who I was had nothing, why not turn into another boy, even if it meant having a stupid name.

Somewhere warm on a plane. Australia. That was the promise. We caught the train to Heathrow. It all happened so fast. 'Dad' at a counter saying he hadn't had a chance to reconfirm or something, but, yes his son was now travelling with him. I had my bag of clothes and my truck. I suppose it looked better for me to have something; I must have looked like a bit of an urchin. He organised everything. He was saying things to people about how sad it was that my mother had passed away. I didn't realise they were talking about someone else, not my real mother, no one would mourn her. I thought I was going through some procedure that must just happen if your mother dies; someone else could simply take you on. Then I remembered we were tricking these people, that even though they didn't look like police, that was effectively what they all were. People to be tricked.

'Dad' scarcely looked old enough to have a 7-year-old son, but he was confident: he had the passports, the tickets and they never looked closely at me in my tracksuit with pyjamas poking out from underneath. I suppose that is what kids travel in, not bowties like in 'my' picture. My accent wasn't like his, but I never spoke to anyone. Perhaps his clipped and refined voice intimidated the officials, or perhaps the papers just seemed so in order that there was no drama. The last thing officials want late at night is a complex problem like a kidnapped child who no one wants anyway. It's the little things they like to flex their muscles over: dates, incorrect forms, uncertain, non-English-speaking foreigners who are easily unnerved and frightened, shy sari-clad Indian women whose packages may look suspicious. There were softer targets around that night for those passport controllers; they weren't interested in a boy and his Dad.

'You must be tired, Vas,' he smiled. 'Why don't you go to sleep while we wait to get on the plane.'

I did this without hesitation, and when I woke he was carrying me down the walkway. His arms were incredibly strong and I felt I didn't ever want to do anything for myself again. Once on board, he curled me up on some cushions and stroked my forehead. 'We're taking off now,' he whispered. I tried to stay awake, but once we were in the air I drifted off to sleep again. The hum of the aircraft, the constant shshshshsh, the smell of the food and my sleepy head in his lap conspired to make me feel like some modern-day *Oliver Twist*, an escapee from the workhouse who could be saved by love. He could be my Dad, he could be my anything.

On that long flight he talked to me lots, told me some of 'the secrets' that I was soon to know off by heart. He reminded me that he was my Dad, that my name was Vas. We dealt with all the 'police' at the Australian end. I looked so tired and crumpled from the trip, my long hair almost obscuring my face, that no one really observed me anyway. By miracle or providence I got to Sydney. Then I went to 'Dad's' house in Paddington and the real story began.

Vaslav Usher. Not bad for council estate white trash. Poor Johnny's surname was Smith – John Smith can you believe. Mum either had no imagination or a very black sense of humour. I suppose I was named for all my real fathers after all. I became Vaslav, named for Nijinsky. Alas, I have failed in the ballet department; I did try but it really wasn't in the blood. I'm okay on the podium of a nightclub but that's about the extent of it.

And my new father? 'Dad' was never really a suitable title. I preferred Shamash. Shamash is an ancient Babylonian God; son of sin, God of Sun, protector of the poor, the wronged and the traveller. It was a title given to him after his portrayal of that very god on a Mardi Gras float, the first float I ever helped on. He was a veteran of many Mardi Gras. That's who I pray to, that's what he was to me.

CHANGELING

Sydney in late spring appeared to me how Disneyland might appear to any child who'd known nothing but poverty – a fabulous impossibility. On one hand I had embarked on a dangerous adventure, losing what precious little I had. On the other, my life turned into a glorious antipodean fairytale. The problem with happy endings in the real world is you can't shut the book on them or put them in a box when things turn nasty.

It was the flowers on the frangipani trees that really sealed my fate. They were the same white and yellow flowers I had seen in my dream, my dream of saying goodbye to Mum.

Sunshine on Vaslav, fresh food and a bedroom specially for me with an *Empire Strikes Back* quilt cover. 'How come? How come?' I'd whisper to myself in the privacy of my room. I'd giggle at how crazy it was, then feel sad that I couldn't show off to anybody. I couldn't show off to my grubby English mates, and kids in Paddington went on planes all the time. I didn't know anyone, so I decided to watch and listen for as long as it took. I hid food and small amounts of money, just in case my dream turned into a nightmare, just in case my handsome prince proved to be an evil sorcerer and the sweet-smelling flowers grew bitter.

There was a nasty loneliness at first, trapped as I was by the knowledge of things beyond me and secrets I was too young to be burdened with. Fables were more real to me than to most kids, who enjoyed their story time in the warm, loving safety of their cashed-up Paddington palaces.

Paddington was like a storybook kingdom: hills and dales, a topsy-turvy of pretty terraces, some huge, some tiny. Houses of every variety on winding one-way streets, secret lanes offering sudden, blinding glimpses of the sunlit harbour and the brightly coloured boats it coddled. Flowers and trees spilling and pushing into any vacant space – a tropical profusion unlike anything I'd seen. Neighbours seemed to be nice to each other and everyone had cars. People knocked gently on the door and asked if a car could be moved or music turned down. Nothing like, 'I've had enough of ya racket ya noisy bloody cow.'

I see it differently now, its wealth and its beauty. Those houses are fortresses these days; bourgeois bunkers, their facades brindled with iron bars, their interiors trip-wired with elaborate alarms. Now I see them as nervous safety zones where neat, athletic women in costly clothes and new BMWs ferry their precious only children to expensive schools, fathers seldom seen. Families who nervously hope the chaos from the next suburb won't venture beyond the Cutler Footway. Perceptions change as we grow, but I loved that momentary perception when I first arrived.

I woke in the mornings with hot sun streaming in on me. I began to eat the strange things prepared for me in the wood-lined kitchen, and abundance mated with greed to put extra pounds on my wiry carcass. With eager curiosity I picked at fruits, green and orange things I'd never seen like kiwi fruit, mangoes, avocado and strong-tasting cheeses not at all like my processed, heat-sealed favourite, which had to be added to the shopping list. Shamash said the kitchen was like a disco because I opened and closed the fridge so often. He had to explain to me that it wasn't proper to eat a little of something and put it back in the fridge. I didn't understand this for quite some time. I was accustomed to doing just that. He said I must cut off a piece, put it on a plate or go in the yard to eat it if I didn't want to use a plate. I could have all I wanted but I was no longer allowed to sit on the floor and eat like a dog. He felt relieved, however. My hunger I'm sure indicated my acquiescence to his proposal of parenthood, and my nervous little body began enjoying the eager offerings of plenty that were being proffered by everyone I came into contact with.

Staging my 'recovery' meant Shamash had to learn to lie thoroughly and convincingly, time and time again. He must have felt like a politician. We defied bureaucracy. Bureaucracy doesn't always work; it may prove a safety net for some and a snare for others. It's a sleepy old web, spun by incumbents who grow used to the 'rule' and who would just as soon process the rare exception as waddle out to the filing room for a different form. You may slip through the net once but when it picks you up further down, there'll be hell to pay from the net above.

Shamash, however, was a brilliant raconteur, able to charm anyone. He told me the story of his real son, and together we wove our own story from it.

Shamash was a dancer. When he was 16 he had won a scholarship to the Royal Academy of Classical Ballet in London. During his time at the Academy, he had an affair with another student, Angelique. She too had great ambitions to dance on the stage at Covent Garden – until she became pregnant. She and Shamash were barely 18 when they became parents, both living in London away from their own parents, and for a time they fooled themselves that they were grown up enough to look after a child.

Angelique, alone with a new baby for much of the day, became obsessed with her weight and would not eat. Her widowed mother refused to help unless Angelique came home to York with the baby, without Shamash. He was dancing, getting better parts with each production, and she resented his success.

There was something else unsettling Shamash – the gradual realisation that he was gay. Poor Angelique was heartbroken. She went back to her mother in York while Shamash stayed a while in London, depressed but dancing still. Ballet was his rise-above-it-all.

After being refused any contact with his son, Shamash

returned to Australia at the beginning of 1977. He was the same age then as I am now.

He joined the Australian Ballet for a few seasons then married his fortunes with David Bergdorf, now one of Sydney's most successful promoters. Together they formed the Bushka Contemporary Dance Company. Following that, Shamash's parents helped him to start 'Potts En Pointe'. It did very well and has continued to do so 'long after our erstwhile corrupt government withdrew their funding for more sinister enterprises' as David would say. He and Shamash were lovers for a while after Shamash came back from London, and they remained best friends through everything that happened.

Life for Angelique became terribly unhappy. She struggled to overcome her anorexia and spent a lot of time in therapy. Then her mother got cancer. Angelique's father had died when she was a child, and though the family had money her mother didn't leave everything to her only daughter. Instead she left a trust fund for Vaslav's education and a small annuity for Angelique. She had been spending her mother's money like there was no tomorrow, which there turned out not to be. She and Vaslav went to Spain and Portugal whenever they could, and because she said she was too ill to stay in England during winter, they spent it in Florida. She finally wrote to Shamash telling him she couldn't cope with Vaslav on her own, that she was suicidal. She wanted him to come and get their child.

Shamash dropped everything, told her he was coming, and booked a return flight. No one knew what she was planning – she had few close friends by then – but as

Shamash was flying over, Angelique and Vaslav drove into Lake Windermere.

The verdict was accidental death, even though relatives in England whispered that it had been intentional. Shamash never wanted to believe that. He was devastated, and he hoped that it had been an accident, though late October was not the time of year to go to Lake Windermere for a picnic, neither was it en route from York to Manchester airport, which had supposedly been Angelique's destination. Angelique's aunt was left to make all the funeral arrangements. Even she didn't know the story.

Over the years, when I asked and was old enough, Shamash would tell me these terrible tales. Fairytales, parables of fogs and autumn leaves, dimly lit country roads with perilously concealed bends. The lady of the lake, an ice maiden always waiting for a clumsy gear change and the sedative-impaired breaking from a ballet-crippled foot that had never graced the stage. In the Autumn stillness the lake had turned screams into gargles; it waited patiently while a small boy struggled vigorously, his roof-thumping and clawing easing into twitching, his soul departing leaving nothing but the fixed gaze of terror, he, alone with his dead mother in a flotsam of cigarette butts from the brimming ashtray.

I dream about that car accident from time to time. I see those white faces trapped behind the cracked glass of the car windows. I swim down beneath that murky, icy water and when I finally glimpse the boy's face, it's mine. He's smiling. I gasp, forgetting I'm in water and then I, too, start to drown, awakening with a horrible start. It's an obvious enough dream for me to have but I hate it. Like many of my horrible dreams, I never know when it's going to strike. I can never save them because I was born from those deaths and their deaths were of pivotal import to my/our story. Brigitte calls it 'residual psychic etching'. I said I don't care what the fuck you call it, I don't like it. She says 'etchings' are the first and easiest dreams to change because they are linked to the past not to the future. She says she'll have me saving them in no time. I can't wait to see how she's going to get me to do that.

Shamash was only in England for a week. Angelique's aunt met him at the airport, where he had been waiting for three hours, and she told him the news. He travelled to York with her and stayed for the funeral, where he received a fair degree of cold-shouldering from the few family members in attendance. The aunt gave him some photos of Vaslav as a baby, set aside with his birth certificate and passport. They were the only things Shamash took.

No family ties there. No mail or photos of Vaslav from Angelique, not many questions from Shamash's parents over those first few years, either. Perhaps they were relieved he escaped England unhitched and without a bastard child to mar their family tree. They never referred to Angelique or the child in all those missing years. It wasn't until Shamash told them that he was gay that they wished they'd taken a little more interest in his former het incarnation. As for me, I was probably beyond the pale. To Shamash's parents I was living proof of Angelique's unsuitability. They didn't know me long enough to ever think otherwise.

Shamash used to say, 'When I saw you with your mother at Victoria Station you must understand how I felt. It was as if God had given me another child; it was too ridiculous a coincidence to be anything else. I have never seen anything like that since, someone just dying like she did. It was a genuine nightmare that whole trip. I was too afraid to phone Mother and Father and tell them about what happened to Angelique and Vaslav. I kept putting it off and putting it off until you were there, offering me the chance to rewrite the rules, change history a fraction, make it just a little more kind, not just to me but to Johnny/Vaslav too. I must have been mad to try it, but we pulled it off didn't we?' We both marvelled at what we'd done; it seemed a miracle.

Probably the most remarkable thing about my being 'reinvented' was dealing with my utter ignorance. I was illiterate, I'd never seen a shower except on telly, had no idea about how to use cutlery, spoke with an almost unintelligible accent. Shamash seemed to understand me okay. He'd lived there, though I doubt he'd got about with anyone quite like Mum and me.

I was a sullen child for quite some time and barely spoke. What utterances people heard from my constantly hung head must have made them wonder what Angelique had been like and if I had such a thick accent it technically ought to have been northern, which it wasn't. When it became apparent that I was illiterate and a year behind at school Shamash would brush it off to his mother with comments like 'Oh Angelique had strange ideas, sent him to the local school which was probably a bad choice, she wasn't with it for the last couple of years, she kept him out of school because she felt too insecure without him' – that sort of thing.

There was always a perplexed aspect to Grandma's dealings with me. I think she favoured the notion that Shamash had been hoodwinked into believing I was his son. The day she had it out with him, in the living room of the Paddington house, I listened, fascinated, behind the door.

'What would you have me do Mum, drown him in his bath and pretend he went down with Angelique? What bloody difference does it make whether he is my son or not? I believed he was mine when she had him, I was there when he was born, I'm on the birth certificate. I rescued him from that crazy family. I don't see your point!'

'All I'm saying Darling is maybe he has special needs, maybe ——'

'Maybe what, Mum? Maybe he won't turn out "right", maybe he won't be "our kind" of Usher? Just leave me to love and bring him up. If you want to help, fantastic, but if you're ashamed of him, like you seem to be of me and my lifestyle half the time, then leave us to it. It's that bloody simple.'

'Nothing is ever *that bloody simple*, Martin. What do you know about bringing up a child?'

'What does anyone ever know before they have them?'

'Most people mix with other married couples who have young families and can discuss the experience – share some of the burdens. I wonder how many of those sort of friends you and that David Bergdorf have?'

'Let's have a go at David, too, will we?'

'All I'm saying is you have a child who's nearly 8, and mark my words most of the behavioural patterns are set by that age, and you're going off half-cocked to bring him up all on your own.'

'Mum, I can only see how I go. I'll get some help if I need it. I've got Thelma. Maybe now I've got a son who'll be at school, I'll meet some of those precious heterosexual couples. Vas's got no real choice; neither do I. I'll join the Gay and Lesbian parenting network.'

'Oh I can just imagine how much use they'll be. You'll be on the phone to your sister and me looking for help long before you get any from that lot. Those women all live on communes and use their own children as social guinea pigs. They won't let the girls wear pink or have dolls, I've read about all these "experiments" – single mothers with no idea what they're getting into, having babies they can't afford on taxpayers' money, bringing up children who will be tormented at school and maladjusted in later life all because the parents were selfish abusers of a system that gives too much leeway ——'

'For Christ's sake, shut up! We're talking about my son, Vaslav. What possible help can this do him? You're like a bloody broken record Mum. If I've heard your views once I've heard them a thousand times. They just bore me, but most of all THEY DON'T HELP ANYONE! What use is anything that doesn't help people? You've tried to teach me that kindness and caution are synonymous, that you can only ever be generous to people who have exactly the same amount of everything as yourself. I don't understand this tough enclave mentality – this wealth you somehow deserve but no one else should be able to access.'

'Your father and I have worked for years to ensure you

and Rosie had everything. You wouldn't have this house in Paddington if your father hadn't organised ——'

'Let's just forget it. The least I can do is try and give Vaslav as many opportunities as I can.'

Grandma made an effort after that, and conceded I was a 'dear little chap'. She seemed to get used to my being around on Shamash's rare visits to the North Shore.

Grandpa, when he wasn't reading the financial papers, would look up and say, 'How's the young fella?' as I wandered past on the way to the pool in the back garden. I desperately wanted to learn to swim, and to everyone's surprise I had no fear of water. I wanted to go in that pool whenever we went to Grandma's. Even when it was cold I'd beg to go in. Grandma would say, 'It's freezing', meaning it was 18 degrees or something. Shamash would say, 'He's from England Mum, this'd be a hot day in England, hey Vas.' I'd giggle, not because it was true but because my life had done this somersault, and there I was with people fussing over my needs, my opinions and my care. And although I had a huge amount of changing to do, there was no doubt in my mind, even after a couple of weeks, that I had landed on my feet, that Shamash was everything he'd seemed, that I was to be looked after and life would be better.

I suppose no matter what Shamash's parents thought of me, their sympathies were with me as I had lost my mother – in both versions of the story. My tale, Angelique's tale and Vaslav's tale were told and told; they were our secrets and there is intimacy in that sort of secret. I always knew the truth but Shamash wove it into both myth and secret, and somehow I became the guardian of both. It is possible to learn a lie, to actually believe it, to rewrite history. Somehow I have a memory of that car going into Lake Windermere, of the jaws-of-life descending to save me but alas not my 'mother'. Shamash and I went there on our last trip back to England. He took me so he could finally lay Angelique and the real Vaslav to rest. From then I was able to mentally picture my second birth as it were. We never went back to Brighton though, to the estate. Shamash offered to take me but I had no interest. Lake Windermere is a prettier place, both to die and to be born; it has worked its way into my 'dreaming'.

Shamash talked to me for hours, trying to work out my interests. He'd take me to book shops and let me have whatever books I wanted. If I showed any interest in trucks, then he'd buy me lots of trucks. If I wanted fish and chips we'd go up to Oxford Street, sit in the park and have them. We'd look in shops which had better things in them than I'd ever seen and because I was with Shamash the shop ladies were nice to me as well: 'How's he liking Australia?' 'Would you like some cake, Vaslav?' None of your 'Get out o' here ya thieving rascal.' I didn't even need to thieve; I could have whatever I liked. It was a true precinct for the privileged, Paddington was, an eye-opener to this little guttersnipe.

Shamash organised private tutors to come to the house. To his great surprise (and mine) I wasn't an imbecile or even especially slow, and let's face it I was hardly what you'd call a winning ticket in the gene pool lottery. Who knows, maybe Mum shagged one of the great minds of England when she was 16 or just, momentarily, snagged herself a cabinet member nosing around the council estate. Perhaps some brainy social commentator was checking the garbage disposal facilities around the back and she happened to be lurking near the piles of old *Sunday Sports* and *Daily Mirrors*. Bingo, an IQ over a hundred, a few brain cells that didn't get clogged up with the fat from the chips. My Mum never got to be a page three girl but perhaps she conceived me on top of one.

It hardly matters now what my seminal source was. I exist, and my slow but absolute foray into Sydney society was under way. Shamash was very popular socially; he had influence, he knew all the 'right' people: curators, actors, artisans. It was names, Darling, names, at our place. None of them meant anything to me back then of course but our house was always full of music, dance and beautiful women with red lipstick and husky voices; alive with the jangle of heavy jewellery, the billowing of extravagant white curtains and clinking of ice in glasses. Expensive, exotic perfumes and *après rasages* mixed with the jasmine and frangipani that blew in from the garden. A spell was cast on all who entered. The golden dancing boys, waxed and polished, with faces to torture the gods, bodies to punish the saints. Theatre directors and their entourages of thespian hangers-on, the voices of the exquisite and the effete echoing through the halls of the Shadforth Street house. I hid from all the grand, urbane confidence that visitors delighted in displaying. It was scary, at first.

People came and went; there was always champagne, always delicious things to eat and always pampering for me. '*Poucet*' became my nickname. 'His father's son,' people would say in big, mock-macho voices. 'A chip off the old block, wouldn't you say, Shamash?' Shamash would laugh discreetly. But I'm jumping ahead.

Thelma, the housekeeper, came in two or three days a week. She always complained cheerfully about the mess she had to clean up, but she was matronly and kind, and wended her way around the banter that used to chortle through the place. 'Thelly,' David Bergdorf would say, 'you've been drinking all the gin again. Shamash, you'll have to fire Thel, she's suckin' down all your gin, mate.'

Thel would stand in the hall with her hands on her hips, smiling dryly. 'We all know who drinks all the gin around here, Mr Bergdorf. My God, when I think about the sort of tax write-offs humble charwomen like me are subsidising with your gin. Martin writes it all off on entertainment, and your gin consumption would form the better part of the national deficit I should say.'

Shamash would dash past, half-dressed, and give her a peck on the cheek. 'We all know Thelly only likes a sherry, don't we Thel? And never more than two a night, isn't that right? And once in a while when there's a *cause célèbre* we can tempt her with a glass of bubbly. I would trust Thelma with my last drop of gin, not so, you, my dear friend.'

Thelma quickly took on the mantle of 'nanny'. It wasn't originally part of her job but Shamash was glad of her help. 'You know my kids are just about big enough to look after themselves and now I get a new boy to start on. We'll have to be friends, Vaslav, because Martin's out at all hours and you'll be stuck with me.'

It was typical of Thel to see a need, roll up her sleeves and get involved. She loved kids, and I'm glad she took to me and that she loved me as she did. If Thel didn't like you she made no secret of it. She had two kids herself: Jeff was already grown up, but Dianne used to play with me when she occasionally came to work with her Mum. She was four years older than me, so she could boss me around a bit. She'd ask me about England and I had to be careful what I said. She also made it clear to me that my Dad was different from other Dads. 'I bet you don't know what a homosexual is,' she'd say teasingly. If she'd said poofter, I might have guessed, but then I accepted everything. Poofter was not a term to be scared of yet.

After my first year of adjusting, I enjoyed my Sydney childhood. From the Paddington house I would go over the Bridge to play for hours in my grandparents' pool, having painstakingly learnt to swim. I had one aunt and uncle who had no children. They were not close to Shamash at that stage, he being a little too arty, I think, for his stockbroker brother-in-law. Rosie was two years older than Shamash, and somehow I don't think she thought it was right, him having a son. She wanted kids but was never able to have them. She was nice to me and looked after me sometimes, but I preferred to go to Thelly's in Homebush or David's in Elizabeth Bay. David always spoilt me, and he had a dog. Homebush reminded me more of where I came from, and I could smell the biscuit factory from Thel's house.

I was okay at school, although the other kids in my class were a year younger than me. There was a tiny stigma attached to this because it may have meant I was dumb. The teacher in my first year had judiciously explained to my class that this was because English school terms were different:

'Vaslav, would you like to tell the other boys and girls about your school in England?' 'Vey're just like 'em ones you got 'ere Miss.' The entire class would erupt with laughter. I spoke as little as possible until I'd got rid of my accent, helped by coaching from Shamash. Sometimes I'd get angry at people trying to change me but then I didn't like the teasing at school.

Shamash was affectionate, though cautiously at first. He would give me a kiss and a cuddle, he'd tousle my hair and sometimes pick me up by my feet and hang me upside down, saying, 'Vaslav the rascal wants hanging out to dry.' We discovered wizzies, and there was just enough room in the back garden for him to do them without scattering the pots of geraniums.

He bought me ballet shoes so I could go into the front room, which was fully equipped with a mirror and barre, and try to copy his steps. I watched him each day like most boys watch their dads shave. Shamash could do extraordinary things with his legs. He'd show off. 'C'mon Vas let's work on your *demi-plié*. Get those legs up to the barre.' It was too high of course; apart from stints on nightclub podiums years later, none of that early training amounted to much. I'm sure the only reason I've been invited to dance in Mardi Gras shows is because I am the son of 'the great one'; everyone says it's not what you know but who you know. I liked watching him; he was a sight to behold. My favourite thing was when he picked me up and twisted me around his head, just as he did with the girls on stage.

When the movie *Flashdance* came out, he used to sneer at it but he could do the dance to 'Maniac'. I'd beg him to do it; I'd bring in water so he could flick it off his head like Jennifer Beals did in the movie. He used to tickle me and say, 'You're just a little steel town girl on a Saturday night aren't you?' I'd squeal and say, 'I'm not a girl, I'm not.'

'A steel town Vas tickled half to death, that's what you'll be when I've finished with you.' He'd tickle and tickle, singing 'What a Feeling' until I was flushed and exhausted on the couch, feeling a little bit like heaven, feeling I was adored. Shamash would leap off down the hall on those legs of his, swollen musculature bulging out of the leotard every which way, singing the theme to *Fame*.

At night Shamash would read stories to me. Sometimes he'd take me to the ballet, often carrying me up to bed from the car, me, already asleep. I loved the luxury of the Opera House and the State Theatre. I decided I wanted to do something in the theatre, and Shamash bought me puppets and a toy theatre. I thought I was too shy to have ever acted or performed, and I imagined painting sets, doing lights or pulling the cords that opened the curtain. I was so disappointed when I discovered they were mechanised. The one in my puppet theatre would lift with one string or draw open with the other.

It was from my private puppet shows that Shamash came to know some of my earlier childhood. I could show him things I would never have told him as my knobbly-headed wooden Punch gave himself injections and drank beer in order to beat and hump Judy. Those were the secret shows that only Shamash saw. They were bedtime shows I'd put on when only he and I were home. He understood the importance of these confessions and never stopped them, even when the Johnny puppet was getting 20 pence from Anorak Man. He'd squirm but he knew better than anyone that shows must go on.

The theatre breathed imagination into me, the colours, the sheer spectacle of it. I begged Shamash to take me to everything, even when he had a date. Of course they had performances to put on too. Their shows were much more sophisticated than mine.

Shamash would go out looking fantastic, dressed in fishnet singlets for nightclubs, torn jeans and cowboy boots. For the Opera House it would be an expensive linen suit, or sometimes a dinner suit. He was very vain, I suppose, but he was also exceptionally beautiful.

The dates had their ultimate destinations, too. Often they would come back to our place, the babysitter (usually Thelly) would go home, and the dates, drinks in hand, would be led up to Shamash's room. He would put on some music in there – Yello was always a favourite, or Grace Jones – and they would do what dates do. Sounds of this sort were familiar. Somehow they represented safety to little *Poucet*. Shamash always closed the door, but he had an old-fashioned lock, without a key. Trembling, I would view his nighttime choreography, and I grew to love it as much as the morning work out. I liked the sudden, secret things the men in there said to each other, words like fuck, cock, arse. Rude words Shamash would never have said to me. In there he'd say them in a different voice, his special voice. Mum had one of those voices, too. She had only used it once in a while, but I remembered the tone; the whore's child's lullaby. The men with Shamash would whisper back, in even lower voices, and I pined for that hotness, that secretness, that nakedness. I wanted my body to grow quickly; I no longer wanted to be a child with toys and books and dumb old things. I, too, wanted to be a *slave to the rhythm*.

Those were hot times in Sydney, the early eighties, just before AIDS. People got pretty carried away in bedrooms in Paddington and Darlinghurst, and Shamash was no puritan when it came to the nocturnal ballet of the flesh. Nor did he shy away from the powders that enhanced the dance. He snorted amyl, sometimes coke, and I learned, through the keyhole, that those smooth arses I had early memories of could be pounded into just as easily as they pounded in. I also learned that drugs were not necessarily a staple diet, not necessarily addictive, not wholly undesirable. I knew that the 'best people' did them as well as the 'worst'. Monkey see, monkey do. If it happens at the bottom you can be sure they're doing it at the top.

MELTING
ICE

Oxford Street. An escape from the suburbs or a ghetto for local inhabitants? A crowded, stacked hierarchy of venues. Not just physically, but socially. It starts underground with sex clubs, dark cavernous gobs that breathe a fetid promise of sordid excitement or drunken relief onto the busy street. Stained chipboard partitions offer yawning holes, the faceless thrill of hot, uvular sensations from the other side. A lucky dip or a game of Russian roulette, indiscriminate mouths offering indifferent supplication. It's a sport not for the faint-hearted, a TAB where all patrons are punters and all cats are grey. Upstairs peep shows proffer bleary-eyed boys with bad skin and reluctant erections. They are yours momentarily for a coin through the cloudy glass divide.

Golden boys from yesteryear wearily dispense condoms and lube carelessly wrapped in Payless paper napkins, tattooing you with a rubber stamp of Bart Simpson as you enter, should you wish to return later, should the current selection prove too grim and a few more drinks be required before carnal agendas can be met. Dry venues, wet venues, peep shows and dingy bars compete like sideshows in a fairground while ATMs that have never known deposits pump out the cash that oils the cogs of this crazy ferris wheel.

At street level the bars purvey the internal lubricants necessary to keep the endless carnival alive. Each bar, pulsating with the flashing of strobes, the constant doof, doof, doof of complex remixes. Songs you know, but you can never remember who sings them. Old favourites redone by some forgettable new studio outfit wearing impossible fashions and sped up until they sound like chipmunks. Songs about following the rules of life, about trying me out or strapping me on, about the rhythm of the night, about swearing on the Bible or about the real me coming alive. Sometimes they're about missing someone like a desert misses rain. I can't help it if, after a few drinks, some of the songs seem to be speaking to me.

At the top of the hierarchy, looking down on it all, are the cocktail bars. Precincts of the most posed and beautiful men, the most worked out, tanned, waxed, designer-singlet-clad bodies you could see. Girls who look like they've just walked off the set of an Aaron Spelling production, heels as high as you like, personas they've invented, beauty at play, sex awaiting consent and jewellery that looks cheap but isn't. They all drink the prettiest, most luridly coloured, most expensive and most alcoholic drinks. The price of one of those drinks would get them into two of those dark clubs.

Three of those cocktails usually ensures that punters end up at one or more of them and that the next day will see the DKNY T-shirt and the Frontier Aviator trousers in the wash or off to the drycleaners. The street seems to know this, it feeds off it and at 3 in the morning attitude seems to vanish. The girls have gone home or to dyke bars or straight venues, and with a carnal flourish from the gods of depravity, a tenuous egalitarianism returns. Then, quietly, unified desires foster a momentary brotherhood in some dark nether world.

The street's glamour is its people, not its architecture – girls and boys strutting, preening and drinking. The boys roam from bar to bar, every muscle of their beefcake bodies accentuated by their child-sized T-shirts. Wind-up boy dolls who know instinctively how to move when they hear the doof, doof of that music. Boys who go to great lengths to look gorgeous and masculine only to throw all 'manhood' away when they mouth the words of campy songs like tribes of drunken high school girls. They are pornography going somewhere to happen. Love them or hate them, come Saturday night, gay or straight, no one wants to miss out on the show.

When you're one of them, you want to stay that way. You don't want to grow old, maybe you don't even want to grow up. But if it is, like some of those 'experts' say, an arrested stage of development, I wish it could have been me who was arrested, not Shamash. You see, no one knew he wasn't really my father, and we both knew it wouldn't have helped matters if they had.

Brigitte knows. Even though I started out just another client of Brigitte's, she doesn't charge me for my visits any more. She says, 'You just come and visit me whenever you feel like it, Darl.' Her house, Misty Rise, is just around the corner in Forbes Street. She's got wind chimes on her balcony, and whenever I go there I feel relaxed. She's very mystical, Brigitte; she knows heaps of weird stuff that she goes on about all the time. It doesn't make all that much sense to me mostly, but sometimes she says things that do. She analyses dreams and seems to know what you're thinking. I don't want to do any of that past life regression – no way – but she did plot my astrological chart, and what she said about me from that made me think there was some order to things. She's quite psychic; she says forget about God and all those other concepts. Before I can even imagine such things I've got to start with learning to love myself. All that stuff sounds wanky, and to be honest it freaks me out a bit.

'Vaslav if you don't clean up that bedroom of yours I'm going to tell Martin I'm resigning, and then where will you be?'

I'd be sitting in there with more toys and books than most other kids, and Thelly'd say I was spoilt.

'You shouldn't keep buying him things, Martin, until he learns how to put them away. It's like a foxes' lair in there.'

'Did you hear what Thel said, Vas? No more books, toys or clothes for you until it's all cleaned up. Now scoot.'

We were sitting in the lounge with the TV on. Shamash was doing some book work and I was watching *Dark Crystal* on video. Already I wanted to watch *Dallas* or Shamash's tape of *Whatever Happened to Baby Jane?* Thelly must have wondered about my tastes. She'd heard David's Bette Davis impersonations and never failed to chuckle at them. 'I was never a Bette Davis fan, even back in the fifties. I always thought she was a battleaxe. I was more your Grace Kelly or Janet Leigh fan,' Thel would say when they started talking about movies. Shamash would smile. 'See David, Thel's got style. She was a Hitchcock girl not a B-grade-fifties-anything-to-save-Bette's-failing-career type movie goer.'

'Style shmile. Give me a woman who can smoke 60 fags a day, drink a bottle of bourbon and still handle one of those huge black Buicks with tears in her eyes while the wipers beat off torrential rain.'

'Well, off you go David. She's holed up somewhere in America. She's in her 80s, had a couple of heart attacks and as many strokes but I believe she's single,' said Thel. 'She might have been an idol to "your lot", but she wasn't someone we girls modelled ourselves on back then. Perhaps I should have been a tougher bird in the bad old days. Could have saved myself considerable grief.'

David and Shamash would look at each other. They loved Thelma's secret, tragic, past. David was always trying to find out more, but they both loved her too much to ever really push her for details.

Shamash wasn't particularly censorious about television but would get 'proper' kids' films for me which I also liked sometimes. I'd put up such a fight over *Dallas*, which was on after my bedtime, that Shamash had started to tape it for me. Thel didn't particularly approve of a child coming home from school to watch such an adult show. She never said anything to Shamash, however, until the day she discovered an explicit magazine under my bed. Thel confronted us both with it in a way that embarrassed Shamash. I could see the colour rise in his cheeks.

'You'd better put these away more carefully, Martin. They're appearing in other quarters.'

He grabbed the magazine from her, and they went into the kitchen. 'Jesus, Thel, a quiet word might have done, don't you think?'

'You're going to have to watch that one, Martin. He's got the makings of a right terror.'

'Have not!' I yelled from the living room.

'And big ears, too,' continued Thelly over the din from the TV.

After she'd gone for the day Shamash said to me, 'Vaslav the snoop should play with his own toys, in his own room, thank-you very much. What do you want with these magazines at your age?'

'Nothing.'

'Well then, why steal them?'

'Dunno, the pictures I s'pose.'

He left the discussion there and wandered out of the room. His face wore an expression that seemed to say, 'I'd laugh if this wasn't for real.'

It took quite some time after that before I found his stash again. He'd pulled out the drawers in his built-in robe and hidden the magazines underneath. I'd wondered, late at night, why I could hear him fiddling with the wardrobe, trying to get the drawers back in. A hiding place, I concurred during one such nocturnal disturbance.

I turned 10 in 1984. AIDS was a whisper then – a rumour, a monster we hoped lurked only in America, like UFOs, trailer parks and serial killers. But it turned out to be real, and by 1984 people could be tested for it. David and Shamash talked about having a test. Both, miraculously according to them, were negative. I hardly knew what it was all about, just that it had to do with sex, and that it was dangerous.

The champagne and gin still flowed at parties, the marijuana smoke still wafted through the house, but the chatter turned to more serious things. To viruses and contagion, to fear, to conversations about 'staying off the scene for a while', then black laughter when someone's voice answered, 'I think that might be a case of too little too late, Love. Talk about closing the stable gate after the horse has bolted.'

The big party event at Shadforth Street that year was the surprise bash Shamash insisted on organising for his parents' thirtieth wedding anniversary. He got caterers in and had a huge ice sculpture of a swan made. Inside the ice sculpture was their present, and no one could depart until it was revealed.

There were dozens of phone calls to plan everything, and I was under the strictest orders to keep the event a secret. Shamash and Rosie revealed their true socialite natures when these sorts of preparations were called for.

'What do you mean waterlilies are not in season? Mum had them for her bouquet thirty years ago. If she could get them then I don't see why we can't have them now . . . If I can't get them in Double Bay where else should I bloody well try? Hopeless, hopeless.'

Shamash was facing a similar *dénouement* with the ice sculpture, which he couldn't store anywhere cool. The caterers wanted to deliver it at 5, he didn't want it until after 7. Thelly muttered to me, 'They're worse than both their parents put together.' Rosie and Shamash, walking past carrying the leaf for the dining table, laughed, 'We are both our parents put together.'

They did their parents proud that night. Shamash stopped bitching about all the North Shore bigots he had to put up with for his parents' sake ('They hate Asians but they love Asian food, they love expensive labels but hate the faggots who design them'), and Rosie finally got her flowers after another round of phone calls. When the guests arrived it was charm, charm and more charm. All Shamash's threats to do an Auntie Mame and serve pickled rattlesnake never came to fruition. As Rosie said, 'If we can't get lilies in Double Bay, I don't like your chances with rattlesnake.'

Surrounded by all the food and decadence, the guests relaxed and enjoyed themselves. Shamash always said apparent wealth was the best antidote to North Shore prejudice, anyway: 'Put 'em in a dinner suit or a Carla Zampatti frock and they usually keep themselves nice.' For a lot of them, visiting the Eastern Suburbs was quite a bohemian adventure. Even if 'parking was a nightmare'.

'Paddington is gorgeous, but we could never give up our view of the Spit,' said one heavily made up 'old friend' as she winked at me.

'Well you know Martin, he was always the arty one, always drawn to the East, weren't you Darling. I thought that anthem of yours used to say "Go west".'

'It did, Mum. They meant San Francisco. You want me to move to Perth or Parramatta?'

'I want you to stay right here in Paddington with Vaslav.'

Grandma drew us both to her as her eyes became dewy. She was getting a bit drunk and sentimental. Shamash refilled her glass shamelessly, and Grandpa said, 'What are you doing to your mother?' Rosie laughed. 'Martin can still do it. He was the only one who could ever get Mum pissed when we were on holidays or out. You used to top up her glass all the time, you horror.'

'Always best to get drunk at the hands of a man who's not going to take advantage of you.' Grandma paused for a second, realising the implications of this, then shrugged and smiled.

'I remember that bottle of Pimms your father took out when we first met. We were just going out for a picnic, and he brought "hard liquor". He pretended it was chivalrous that he remembered to bring a lady's drink. There was I, Miss Post-War Picture Perfect with my home-cooked cold cuts in a basket and a trifle for God's sake, and he's pouring me Pimms and lemonade – more Pimms than lemonade mind you – from this ancient ice box his mother had stored out in the garage.'

Grandpa was laughing too, his eyes lighting up in his foxy old face as I'd never seen them before. 'The best part is poor old Mum thought I was being a real gent "taking a picnic". I told her I'd been down to the grocers and bought everything we needed for a picnic and I'd strapped the old icebox on the back of the car. "Let me have a look, Love," she said. "I'll see what you've left out. You can't leave packing a picnic to a fella." Well, I wouldn't show her. I said she'd either like what I bought or she'd do without.'

'We shouldn't go on,' said Grandma. 'Rosie and Martin have heard this a dozen times.'

'A million times, Mum,' said Rosie. 'But we love it all the same.'

'And there's a tiny bit more revealed with each new telling,' said Shamash, who was swirling his wine in his glass like some arch troublemaker, his father's foxiness somehow reflected in his own eyes.

'Well, Bob had that useless old Austin that you had to crank start – we're talking 1951 mind you,' she said as a general aside, 'and this great icebox strapped on the back. He'd put a huge lump of dry ice in there so every time it was opened we were engulfed in a cloud. I thought it was madly romantic, and before I knew it I was quite tiddly.'

'Oh Love, you were pissed.'

'Bob! Vaslav's here,' Grandma said in mock rebuke.

'He'll hear worse than that if he lives in this house, won't you young fella?'

I nodded, smiling like a reborn angel who'd never heard dirty talk. 'Dad and David say worse on the phone.'

'That's enough, Mr Tattle Tale,' said David.

Grandma was settling back in to the memory. 'A girl had to know how to handle herself on the Pimms.'

Everyone laughed and stared at the light refracted through the dripping centrepiece as I watched grown-ups toasting the years – years I couldn't imagine. Shamash played the handsome, successful son and Rosie, the pretty, well-to-do daughter. I finally got to wear the bowtie I'd never had before, and the family photo taken on the balcony that night looked, for all the world, like a royal one. It could have appeared in *Harpers*.

I loved the clothes and colour of Shamash's world. I may have been trash once but my value had gone up beyond my wildest dreams. I was like those over-valued houses in Paddington, the ones that ended up having mortgages worth more than their resale value when the recession came. Shamash was over-capitalising on me.

The anniversary present that was finally revealed when the ice sculpture melted was two first-class tickets on an exclusive chartered flight to Antarctica, a flight that took only 50 passengers. Grandma and Grandpa had talked of taking one of these trips, and Shamash had thought that to give the present in such a fashion would be ingenious.

It would have been if that flight hadn't crashed.

How strange are some of the twists in Shamash's life – how he found me, how he made me his son, and how he lost his parents against similar odds. He and Rosie had to come to terms with the devastating fact that it was they who had bought the tickets that killed their own Mum and Dad.

Shamash was quite religious in his own way. He seemed to rage against God; it was like opera. I felt strangely remote from the grief, as if it were a nuisance. I felt angry that the crash upset Shamash so much, but I couldn't feel that I'd lost real grandparents. A pall settled over the Shadforth Street house that summer. Shamash lost interest in his dancing and David cast shows without him. Rosie phoned him often: 'For God's sake, Martin, it was an accident. You know they wouldn't blame us. You can't keep doing this to yourself. We'll have to manage somehow. I thought you were the strong one.'

I couldn't count on Shamash's moods then, not for quite a while. He was never cruel to me, though he was sometimes distant. I would go into his room at night and cuddle him. When he was crying he would wrap himself around me and rock me, or himself, to sleep (I was never sure whom the rocking was for). 'Don't you ever leave me, Vas,' he'd say. 'Don't you get yourself killed. If anything happened to you I don't think it would be worth it anymore, do you know what I'm saying?'

He'd come good sometimes: 'I don't suppose a proper dad's meant to cry like I do.'

'So what if you do? It doesn't matter.'

'You don't think I'm an old sook?'

'Nah, I was pretty sad when my Mum died. You're the best person I ever got.'

'You think so?'

'Course. Reckon I was a lucky kid to get the best dad ever – 'specially on a railway station.'

He'd cuddle me close and tell me I was the one sure thing in his life. I don't think I understood the depth of his misery then. Childhood refuses to know misery, it floats above, wondering what it must be like, waiting, one day, to find out.

Shamash was probably too consumed by his own grief to know how much I needed him. When we lay together like that, sometimes all night, he didn't notice how absorbed I was by him. He didn't notice how I stroked his back, how I buried my face in his chest, how the deep breaths I took when I was so close to him were to smell him, not to breathe. Big smells of Shamash, taking some of him inside me. It wasn't just the Eau Sauvage in Summer, the Jazz in winter, it was the essence of him, the mannish smell I didn't produce yet.

How do we know exactly the right way to love someone? What is childish sensuality and sexuality? We imagine that somehow it just comes into being some time, conveniently, around the age of consent. But we all know that the cool and naughty kids start bonking as soon as someone else is prepared to do it with them. The whole world is turned on by young lovers. What's wrong with exploring the parameters a bit earlier?

By the time I was 11 my hormones were working overtime. I was deeply in love with Shamash, deeply in lust. I would bury my head in his clothes, especially his more intimate garments like leotards, underwear. He had a G-string, and the mere look of it excited me. The smell of him in the toilet brought on 'grown up feelings', and a tissue he had masturbated onto and been careless about disposing of I sniffed and tasted. When I lay with him, when I was sure he was asleep and the warm nights kept us uncovered, I could sneak my tongue under his arm and, if I was very bold, I could taste other parts as well. I suppose even if he had woken up he would have been too embarrassed, too incredulous to comment on this sort of behaviour. He would have put it down to an untameable wildness.

As that sad summer came to an end, Mardi Gras suddenly became a focal point as it did each year. This time David wanted me on the Potts En Pointe float. Shamash objected at first.

'He's already getting teased at school about all the ballet shit, and if he goes on the float it'll be worse. Why don't we wait a couple of years, Dave, then see if he wants to?'

'A couple of years! He will be positively adolescent. I know adolescence is not without its charms but we must have the child, the son of Sun and Sky, Quetzalcoatl. They're all characters from the Americas this year, Shamash. Won't the Festival of Light adore a 10-year-old child adorned only in a glorious sheath of gold and magenta with feathers. We need a child to lend a *Satyricon* decadence to the whole shebang.'

Shamash didn't take too much convincing, and I didn't care if I got teased at school. I was sure the other kids would envy me riding on a float like that.

'You'll have to dress him in silver. He's too pale to wear gold.'

'Nonsense,' said David. 'We'll put fake tan on him, and he will ride on the highest point of the float. Gods and princes can get away with lamé at any hour. And Vaslav is a prince, aren't you, Hon?' David pinched my cheek.

Shamash picked me up and hung me over his shoulder, saying, 'Prince of messes and half-full bowls of Rice Bubbles in the dishwasher is what he's prince of this week. I'm trying to teach him to fly, Dave, but can't quite get the take-off happening.' He had me suspended on both arms and was turning around like an amusement park ride.

64

'Perhaps he's broken,' offered David.

'That'd be right, and the warranty's just expired. Isn't that always the way?'

'You could put him in the dishwasher, that might fix him,' said David, his finger to his mouth as if he were nutting out scientific possibilities.

'You're absolutely right! It said something in the manual about cleaning boys in preparation for flight – *A clean boy offers less particle resistance and can thereby soar at much higher altitudes.*'

'Boys can't fly, you dicks,' I said, giggling and pummelling Shamash's back. 'And I don't want to go in the dishwasher.'

'How do you know? You've never even tried. You could try to catch all those Rice Bubbles that are still in there.'

'Yuk, all soggy mush.'

'Not true Vaslav, they bake on hard as porcelain in the final cycle, and we know how Thelly likes that, don't we?'

And on it would go, he and David treating me more like a kid brother than a son. 'You take the ankles, I'll take the wrists – whoever gets the biggest bit can make a wish.' I can't remember who got the biggest bit; it felt so good being tickled and 'pulled apart' that I hoped the tug of war would never end. They wished for the biggest float ever as I lay writhing on the floor, all giggles, flush and erection.

When it came time for the float it was all hands on deck, and I was old enough by then to get some important jobs like painting and *papier mâché* while all those gorgeous boys and girls from the 'dance factory' made a fuss of me. I have photographs of the float, of me waving to an effigy of Fred Nile. I am making the Indian powowowowow noise with my mouth, although I was an Aztec Indian God technically. But I only knew the wild west ones at the time so I behaved as one. Shamash was Lord Con Ticci Viracocha, Prince and Creator of All Things.

I had been to previous Mardi Gras, sometimes with Thelly, sometimes with Rosie. Because Shamash and David were always on board their float, I had always needed minders. This time I was to take my own place. I loved the parade and I loved the drinks at Shadforth Street afterwards. They were a riot of booze, drugs, music and colour.

I guess that year there would have been Madonna's 'Into The Groove'; there was always Heaven 17, Yello and no party went off without serious dance interpretations of Duran Duran's 'Girls on Film'. I was getting a little bold by then, sneaking small glasses of champagne, which I'm sure Shamash turned a blind eye to. A couple of the girl dancers from the company got me up for 'Girls on Film', prancing about pretending they were lipstick cherry models (which they could have been) until I, light-headed from the champagne, started cat-walking too. Shamash, floating on Mardi Gras high spirits and, no doubt, other substances, would pick me up sometimes and give me a huge 'European kiss'. He always said European kisses were more generous than our WASPy little English pecks, our frigid little smackers: 'The mouth is the mark of generosity, it's the initial source of love in all its forms.' A European kiss meant two, and traditionally they landed on each cheek. Shamash always kissed with his mouth open a bit, leaving a touch of wetness on your cheek afterwards. Because I was special, I was a son, I got the most generous kisses of all. He would press his open mouth to my cheeks for seconds that seemed like minutes, and he would whisper into my ear, 'You know which boy I love most in the whole world don't you? You know who is the most beautiful boy?'

They were rhetorical questions, of course, but they were wonderful affirmations, not only of love but of beauty. It must be said, Shamash's world favoured the fair; it celebrated beauty in all its forms.

I don't know that I would be described as beautiful now. At 20 I don't have Shamash's physical grace nor his break-your-heart cheekbones, but had I stayed in the slums I dare say I would have no beauty at all. Perhaps a momentary bout of cuteness, that sort of disposable, use-up-able, cheap sexual beauty that is so ephemeral. The sort of beauty that is fucked out of you very promptly by the urging of hormones and the demands of addiction. It is fucked out even quicker from whores like my Mum, or like I probably would have been had I stayed, had she lived. I suppose somewhere in my twisted aesthetic this idea controls me. The idea that if someone is beautiful inside you've got to fuck it out of them or fuck into them to get to it. The problem is the more we hammer at whatever it is we want to take from each other, the less it is there.

Shamash and I knew we were perched on the most dangerous of social precipices; we knew what was forbidden. If you'd loved Shamash, if you'd known him like I did, if you were a child as hungry as I was, you would have destroyed him too.

I think it happened during a Blancmange song that I was dancing to with the girls. Shamash was swanning around, kissing people, grinding his hips against them, being generous and pretentious. He was still sporting some of his feathers from the parade but had changed into a one-piece garment that looked like a 1920s bathing suit. It was black and white. I still had on my little gold shorts and a feather necklace. Under the fake tan I was flushed from dancing and from the champagne.

Amidst this oom pah pah Shamash incorporated me into his round of affection pouring. He swept me off the floor as only he could and kissed me, wetly, on each cheek. To my surprise, I kissed him back, first on the cheeks as he had done, then on the mouth. Because we were moving, I was suspended in mid-air. I don't think anyone noticed, but I held the kiss on his mouth for a second or two, my mouth open a little as was his. Suddenly I got really bold and stuck my tongue into his mouth. Shamash shrieked, then laughed. He quickly put me down and smacked my bottom, but as I went back to the girls, back to Blancmange, I saw a flicker of concern pass, almost imperceptibly, over his face.

KIDDIE
PORN

Some politician was on the teev last night crapping on about drugs and 'young people'. It was a current
affairs program that kept cutting to the parents of some
20-year-old like me, only this dude had gone to the point of
no return on a 'lethal cocktail of narcotics'. The scene was a
'modest' Pymble home (modesty in Pymble starts at about
350K). The family was tearfully huddled on their pastel
green sofa – Mum, clinging for dear life to a china-framed
picture of her boy, her fingers nervously rubbing the little
ceramic rosettes on the corner, her eyes yielding up big
drops of ratings rain. Dad sat deadpan, holding her hand –
the stoic rock that backs family values. They're trying to
come to terms (on national television) with their son's
wasted life.

The voice-over kept using terms like 'cut off prema-
turely' and 'a tragic ending to a promising young life'. A

vicar who had worked with teenage drug addicts had his ten cents' worth too: 'We don't blame the parents, all too often "these kids" are displaying warning signs which most parents haven't had the experience or education to recognise.' Blah blah blah, and he finished with some purler about the restlessness of youth and its social consequences, 'which more than ever before are pervading all strata of society'. From this they cut to the stock footage of prostitutes and drunks in Kings Cross. Never mind that half the prostitutes up there are old enough to be the vicar's mother and have lived through AIDS and two world wars – well, Vietnam at least.

So they're panning along the street, showing those sad photocopies on poles and in windows – 'Debbie, please come home, we miss you and so do the kids'. The posters are torn, flapping in the breeze like garage sale notices weeks after the event, leaving viewers with the impression that 'Debbie' never has gone home. The picture is of a birthday girl in happier times. Never mind that she could be living in Newtown and has probably changed her name to Ginger or Chinois. Perhaps she has a well-paid job as a receptionist for a leading international airline. Maybe she works as a sales assistant for Priceline and never had to turn one trick when her train arrived from Orange or Dubbo or wherever the fuck.

During this segment they panned the fountain area and who should be sitting there looking out of it but my mate Owen. He looks up, like hey man and then goes to block the camera. I rang him at his rat nest in Glebe and said, 'Man, you were just on TV as a junkie in the Cross.'

'Hey, I know – wicked wasn't it. They gave me 50 bucks to do that a couple of months ago. Man, I needed that money. This guy who was filming couldn't find any junkies. They're all drunks in the Cross – no smack there – so they got me to do that far-out-man look.'

'What if your Mum sees it?'

'She's in Fiji or Vanuatu or some fuckin' place with Dad. Fifty bucks is 50 bucks, eh Vas? Probably one of their friends'll tell 'em. Hey, you got any weed man? How about I come 'round to your house and play? Watcha say we visit Cone Land?'

I looked at the few sprigs I had left in my mull bowl. Knowing Owen, he'd suck them down in one cone. 'Haven't got much,' I say, 'but come if you want. Bring a vid, the TV's crap.'

They shit me these TV shows, but I can't help watching. It's like they think that somehow they could just stop people experimenting with stuff. As if suddenly everyone who lives on the edge – or even people who experiment with drugs or use them for parties and fun – doesn't have a clue what they're doing. That all of a sudden we'll all be saved and safe and aspiring to that 'modest' house on the harbour.

My theory is that there used to be explorers, places to live dangerously in and as human beings we demand a certain dangerous and exploratory terrain. Drugs allow us to do these things in our heads. Sadly these endeavours are not recognised by the powers that be so we don't get highways and mountains named after us. Also, people have to sell what they've got – get out the hairy chequebook. Or sell a story like mine. Right now that's all I've got to sell. Sympathy? I don't need it. Who's going to put me in gaol? It's not me I seek to vindicate. I don't think I need to worry about film rights either, because until there are robot children for movies, no one will touch this story with a barge pole.

Eleven, 12 were crucial ages for me. Hormonally I developed early in that white trashy way that really was my genetic inheritance. I could masturbate and actually ejaculate. Sure, the amount of sperm was negligible, but it was accompanied by that ancient sting, the sensation that drains and somehow saddens us yet must be done again and again. We all become slaves to it, animals for it, and often we are ruined by it. When at last it came for me, I could finally put reason to a life of unexplained depravity. All that grunting and shagging, all those drawers full of lubricant, condoms and stimulants, all my mother's dressing and undressing; everything made sense.

It was for this that people were dying, this was the rhythm of life, this was why some people were 'bad'. Good people tamed it, hid it, offered it up to God or worked it off in the gym. Not me. I knew as soon as I felt it that badness was in the genes, and while this masturbation thing might have been pleasurable and compelling in its own right, the involvement of someone else in the scenario would be heaven. Or hell.

There were other Mardi Gras, and there was the scandal, the unfinished urban myth about Shamash and me. It's a good one, comparable to Lindy Chamberlain and that baby of hers. But ours is more hush-hush. I've been at things where people have been talking about it without knowing who I was. I've watched breathy would-be socialites whisper

72

about me whenever I pass them. People seem to think you don't notice or hear, or they just don't care. 'Look, that's Vaslav Usher. He's still around can you believe it.' Yeah, I'm still around. What do they expect? Should I be dead at 20? Is my mere presence a reminder of an outdated bit of tabloid titillation? Am I supposed to just vanish as soon as they tire of my story?

No one ever mentions it to my face, no one asks me about it. A whole room might be buzzing with Chinese whispers about what 'used to happen', getting more and more lurid with each drink and each telling. Negligent jurors, these, both condemning me and fantasising about me at the same time, all at my expense. They don't care about protecting victims, if that's what I am supposed to be. They just want another freak in the circus, something to recoil at when they read their Sunday papers over a latte in Victoria Street.

I was a sleazy-snoop-about sort of kid. I knew where Shamash kept his pornography. He did try to hide stuff from me but I could sniff out secret spots like a dog. I wonder if he ever guessed that I snooped like I did? He kept drugs hidden too (not that I stole them then, except perhaps a sniff now and again of the amyl). I remembered how I'd been fascinated by some of Mum's more handsome clients and now I could see dozens of even more desirable men in full colour carnal extravaganzas, I began to think that 'this' was the sex for me.

At primary school a girl sparked my het interest for a while. Even at 12 she hinted constantly at seduction; at secret girl mysteries and pleasures, her chest already pushing forward to accentuate the tiny swellings that would become her breasts. In the playground she'd twist herself around metal poles, suspend herself from monkey bars, fidget in ways that would have her dress riding up or catching between her narrow thighs.

In her back garden after school her legs refused to stay still – they drew constant attention to themselves, knees knocking together as if to say, 'Guess what we've got between us?'

'Vas, has your Dad got a girlfriend?'

'Nah.'

'He doesn't like girls, does he?'

'He likes girls enough.'

'My Mum has a boyfriend.'

'So?'

'I've seen them doing – you know – it.'

'I've seen "that" before.'

'Do you like touching girls?'

'S'alright,' I said, thinking it might be worth a try.

'Come with me,' she demanded one afternoon, dragging me down to the garage at the back of the garden. Her skirt dropped to the concrete floor. 'You'll have to pull your trousers down, too.'

We both stood there behind her Mum's car, her white blouse parting like a theatre curtain to reveal a suprisingly swollen little vulva. It pouted in angry contrast to the precocious, delicate frosting of hair, so new, I'm sure it was still astonishing her. At least I had a couple of hairs of my own for her to touch.

I felt inside her and she pulled me close, touching my hard willy. It was meaty and clammy. She started moaning, moistening and going all weird. I tried to imagine what it must feel like. I guess I envied her a bit; I was starting to wonder if she'd let me put my dick in. 'Go on, what are you afraid of?' she growled with startling urgency. I tried to push my dick in, but it was awkward, what with her skirt around her ankles and my trousers and undies. I moved closer, nearly falling on her, then her ankle touched the exhaust pipe on the car, which was still hot. She squealed from the burn and we were forced apart.

Anyway, her Mum called out to us, 'Vaslav, your Dad's on the phone.' We had to dress quickly and go inside before we got sprung. Her secret wetness was still on my fingers when I picked up the phone, her smell adding strange dimensions to a perfunctory phone conversation with Shamash.

I can't relate to all that gay space, men-only, women-only shit. I guess in sexual terms I took the path of least resistance, but I've always gravitated to those sorts of 'bad girls', those sorts of people.

Heterosexuality may have intrigued me, it still does. I guess that's why I'm more queer than anything else because pornography can be any kind and still turn me on so long as the people in it are sexy. I don't like those fat, 50-year-old women with cunts like badly opened tins of sardines, but neither do I like those overweight, balding Scandinavian men, those warty 'cancer Charlies' with hair on their backs and almost visible bad breath, whose only apparent assets are their huge red schlongs which look like they've been scalded in boiling fat and promise all the STDs under the sun. I've got nothing against old people but I wish they wouldn't do porn movies.

75

Pornography haunted me as a kid. With the help of Shamash's magazines I knew everything I wanted to do was actually possible. I showed them to a boy at school. He said my Dad was weird but he still came to the Paddington house, still looked at the pictures, still had a snort of the amyl and still let me work my finger into his arsehole before the dull, thumping flush of the amyl had dissipated. He still uttered in that moment of drugged, slightly masculine and strangely fey passivity, the one word that says it all – *cool*. If you'd ever sniffed amyl you'd know *cool* is the wrong word. *Hot*, I would say, is a more apt description. That was one way of taming other boys, get them to have some sex with you and they'd never turn against you at school again. It's the safest form of childhood blackmail. If I qualify for a PhD in anything in this world, blackmail would be it. When sexuality awakens it refuses to be put back down.

Shamash was no angel; he too was a slave. He took the drugs that made the city look more beautiful, made nights last longer, made boys more desirable and turned strong, almost controllable lusts into ones that must be satisfied at all costs. More so after his parents died. There were more young men brought home, more sheet changes, more signs of disapproval from Thel. Damage alters people that way. It shifts our understanding of justice and sends people to war with God.

The Sleaze Ball is an annual spring rite in Sydney. A Bacchanalian fest of diabolical proportions, an occasion for thousands to frock-up as their wildest fantasy. I was well and truly 12 according to Johnny's (non-existent) birth certificate but only just according to Vaslav's. (People often say I'm more like an Aries than a Virgo; that's because I'm a 'secret Aries' but freakishly I have this Virgo ascendant. Brigitte said the cosmos knew I'd be living most of my life as a Virgo.)

I think that was the first time Shamash went out without me having a babysitter. He must have come in at about 3 in the morning (he never stayed out all night like some). He was buzzing, breathing deeply from some designer drug that had mellowed out. I had been asleep on the floor by his wardrobe drawers, his pornography collection strewn around me. He shook me gently.

'Vaslav, what have you been up to? You shouldn't be going through my drawers mate, they're private. And you oughtn't be pouring over all that shit either, not at your age ... there are reasons why you shouldn't be looking at that stuff, good reasons which unfortunately escape me at this precise moment.'

I did my head-hanging bit. 'I was just ——'

'I know what you were just, you were just having a wank but you've got your own room in which to wank. Kiddo, I'm not going to get mad about it, God knows this is a degenerate enough house in a city that is a moral cesspool, and you my darling boy do not hail from a puritanical background. Far be it for me to try to tame your wild spirit, and I'm certainly not the Festival of Light's model father. Now put them away and call it a night.'

'Can I have a cuddle?'

'Oh Kiddo, I've just been to Sleaze. I'm knackered.'

'Just a little one, Shamash.'

'Alright'.

He had taken off his boots and only had a pair of Lycra shorts on. He collapsed onto the bed and closed his eyes. I cuddled him, and whispered, 'I love you Shamash.'

'I know you do, Kiddo. I love you'n'all, now sleep.'

I didn't, though. He sighed long and deep, like you do on drugs. I saw what those drugs did long before I had them myself. I saw their magic. I was sometimes a victim of the snappiness they produced in the ensuing days but Shamash was a happy man that night. He was smiling like an angel, and he smelt of sweat from dancing, exuding the metallic smell of fake tan. I remember how the fragrance of his deodorant lingered on him, with just a faint hint of Jazz.

There lay my saviour, my Dad, my Shamash; there before me was that physique he seemed almost blasé about. He was smiling because he was tripping, dreaming, enjoying the momentary bliss we all try to get a hold of once in a dance-party while. I knew the way he was feeling he wouldn't resist me running my fingers up and down his back. That wasn't a sexual thing; we did that all the time. That's what tactile, affectionate dads do with their boys.

I did it and he groaned a little, he smiled even more, his eyes staying closed. I did it for a long time, gradually moving to his arms then down to his legs. I gently traced his buttocks and he didn't stop me. As I drew with my fingers down the insides of his legs I noticed them move, ever so slightly, apart.

Gently, he angled one leg out, bending it as he did but remaining on his stomach. He was trying to make it look like a natural adjustment but I knew with a flutter of visceral excitement that he was trying to accommodate an erection under there. If he had opened his eyes, my erection would have been visible to him, straining like a grotesquely adult thing from my child-sized Jockettes. But he didn't; he let me keep stroking him, he pretended he was asleep. I moved to the front of the exposed leg and gently up to the Lycra shorts, then ever so slowly to the bulge that was there. He groaned and so did I. It was drenched, and at my touch a fresh discharge seemed to pour forth. He wasn't smiling any more, he seemed to be bracing himself.

His eyes opened, and it was a different Shamash. There was lust in those eyes, there was anger, and pity and desperation. 'It's not going to be enough to have a dad is it, Johnny. You want more than that, don't you.' He tore his shorts down and his erection slung itself free, glistening like some monstrous prize. 'There, that's it, that's what you want to see, isn't it.' Then, before I could do anything, he choreographed a movement so quick, so beautiful that it remains the most exquisite memory of my childhood. He stood, swung me off the bed and twice around his body, and wrapped me around his head. My dick was in his mouth. I must have cum from that sensation in about five seconds. Shamash coughed as I did, sucked hard one last time, and gave a deep, operatic plea: 'Now will the child be stilled.' And the child was.

He took me to my room, to bed, saying quietly, 'We must talk tomorrow. Privately.' I lay sleepily, almost rapturously in my bed, only half aware of the sobs from the next room. The thing that had happened, the secret danger that excited me most of all was his utterance. He had called me 'Johnny'. He'd never called me that before, and I'd half forgotten about Johnny. He could be someone else, he could be anyone at all. Unlike Vaslav, he could never be tamed or cultured. He was like his mother, hardly a person at all, just someone to do stuff to, something to fuck, a disembodied fantasy, a wordless image in one of Shamash's magazines. Could I do those faces the boys in the mags do while they're being fucked? I was consumed by the desire to 'be pornography', to begin cultivating long lost Johnny. I'd had a glimpse of him in my mind's eye; slouching around the council estate wiv' nuffink better t' do 'van suck a bit o' cock and give it nice ol' bit up the jacksy.

Sunday morning arrived. Shamash never slept late after he had done drugs. He never drank much on those nights and was usually in quite good spirits; it was never until Mournful Monday or Eckie Tuesday that that he got moody. Breakfast was a sombre event that morning though.

'You know we can't talk to anyone about what happened last night, Vas. I shouldn't have done that.'

'Doesn't bother me, what happened, Shamash. I'm glad,' I said. 'I won't tell.'

'You will tell, that's just the thing. Perhaps not next week, not next year, perhaps not for several years but all sorts of betrayals await you; sometimes it seems that's what life is all about. You're trying to get hold of every adult thing you can – too soon. If you do everything too early you'll be sorry, things will seem empty when you're older. It's the nature of being a kid, and I'm not trying to patronise you, honestly. The balance is all wrong for us to have anything like what I think you're fantasising.'

'Didn't you like what I was doing last night? Wasn't it nice?'

'Oh come on, Vas, you're a kid. I'm supposed to be your bloody father. Nice is not a word to use for a situation like this. Not everything I get up to is "nice" for Christ's sake. I want to bring you up right, not let you become some sort of freak, and that's what you would become if I let you grow up at the break-neck speed you seem determined to.'

I refused to look up from my cereal.

He went on, 'It's an awful thing to have to tell you, but the world views what we did last night more harshly than almost anything. And the fact that I can't adequately explain why to you is central to the reason for that taboo. This isn't Ancient Greece, and no offence Vas but I've never gone for kids in the past.' He put his arm around me and tried to pretend everything was okay.

I hung my head, shame mingled with unrequited love. But I also began to realise my power. I was a 12-year-old monster. I was a spoilt brat.

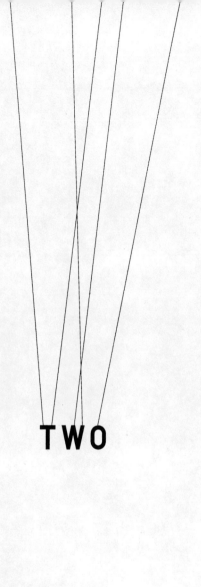

TWO

CHEESE
STICKS

I went to see Brigitte today. She thinks I should record all my dreams, but I'm on Prozac these days so I don't dream very often. I tend to think that the dreams you have on tranquillisers don't really count anyway, and I've been on one thing or another for the last two years. I was taking heavier things for a while – Rohypnols, Valium and various other non-prescription, non-legal shit as well. Brigitte says I shouldn't be on sedatives at my age; she says that if I really was the architect of everything that happened then why is it that I can't cope? Maybe Shamash was right about doing everything so young.

The thing is that sex – the real get-addicted-to-it, have-as-much-of-it-as-you-can-and-use-up-your-youth-because-it's-the-best-sex-asset-you'll-ever-have sex – is a marginal activity. It's seen as delinquent, but there ain't no cure. If I'm a nymphomaniac then fuck the lot of them. It's a victimless crime. I might be marginal, criminal in some ways, but I'm the only victim of my crimes and I'm getting damn tired of everyone's endless interference. 'Get off my case!' I shout to no one in particular and everyone at the same time.

Brigitte's different. She is never shocked by anything. She says, 'I know what you boys are like', with a glint of wickedness flickering in her eye. She's the sort of woman people might call a fag hag if she weren't a dyke. She hasn't got a girl right now, though she reckons she's looking. She's quite old, about 45 or something, but she doesn't look it. Not that that's really old or anything, but she's the first older friend I've made for myself.

Somehow she's beyond all the politics of sexuality. She's not like some of those Newtown dykes, but she's not a bullshit dyke either. She's flying out there in the cosmos somewhere, but still has her feet firmly planted on the ground. She says men are by far the more fragile of the sexes egotistically: 'Their mothers put one foot wrong during childhood and all womankind pays for it the rest of our lives, God help us.'

She sounds like Thel sometimes. Thel had this husband who used to hit the bottle and really knocked her around from time to time: 'I was a fool to love him as long as I did but I had two young kids, and you men'll never understand what that's like. Ten years where I had no choices. I had to stick with him until the kids were both at school and I could get a job and give him his marching orders.'

Brigitte's more mysterious. It's no use asking her how she got enough money to own Misty Rise; she'll just tell you some bullshit about channelling it out of the cosmos or something. But there are pictures of her with an older man, and she refuses to adhere to the reigning lesbian philosophy that rules men out completely as lovers: 'When you get to my age love needs to be more spiritual, the body ain't what it used to be.' When I press her for her history she just says it's another land in which she doesn't travel.

She has theories about everything, and sometimes I like to hear them: 'A lot of promiscuous men pretend they're fetishising masculinity, celebrating the "wholeness" of there being other males like them. They imagine for themselves a fraternity of endless male companionship and eroticism, not realising that the very structure of that society is its own downfall. It becomes like some endless hunting trip – the weather turns cold, it rains, the tent leaks, they run out of cartridges and want to go home, but it's too late.'

I think about some of the old queens who hang out in bars all the time; it's hard to imagine they were ever my age.

I don't know why Brigitte tells me all this, it's not like her lectures are going to make me turn around and behave myself. And I'm not political at all. I don't think I'm a misogynist either, but it's like how everyone thinks all queers are child molesters, or how they think gay men are misogynists and all dykes are man haters or ball breakers. I suppose it's just because we don't fuck girls. I've never thought of myself as a misogynist but I remember Shamash coming back from an all-male dinner party one time and saying to someone on the phone that he'd commented at the table, 'What I hate most about Sydney is all the misogynistic queens.' Apparently there was an embarrassed silence and

Shamash realised suddenly he was not with like minds. When no one said anything he added, 'Tonight's hosts and any future Potts En Pointe financiers excepted, of course.' They'd all laughed after that. I remember him saying to Rosie that the nastiest bitches in this town have got balls, and she'd answered, 'You haven't worked for some of the women.'

Shamash used to go on about all the problems of 'coalitionist politics'. I didn't even know what he meant at first. He said poofs and dykes move further and further apart: 'You might get young gays agreeing with young dykes about issues like pornography and censorship at university but give them a decade and you'll find gay men are just too caught up with the rigours and demands of their sexuality to be really focused on lesbian agendas. Ours (gay and lesbian) is an arranged marriage, but that's as it should be. For all the leftist politics you'll hear espoused from gay and lesbian social advocates, at the end of the day gays and lesbians, like all subcultures and minority groups, are necessarily xenophobic. We need each other for protection if nothing else.' He said good things come from that need.

It's weird when I think about stuff he was involved in, stuff that went right over my head, apart from one line that made sense: 'Don't ever think the world would be a better place if it were run by fags and dykes, Vas. Power works out the same whoever gets it. It is far too hard to acquire and too intoxicating, when obtained, not to corrupt.'

Well I've got fuck-all power though I'm often intoxicated, and it seems to me that it was people who had the power that decided I was corrupted. All these theories don't seem to count for much when I look at the shambles Yours Truly Prince of Messes has made for himself.

Sometimes it seems like everything is to do with sex, but Brigitte says that's specifically my dilemma. I just want out of thinking a lot of the time. With Prozac you can't get quite as out of it; you can't take two or three if you want to go out to a party or a rave or something. What I tend to do is go off it for a few days then take something substantial like an E or two and follow them up later with a Rohy. That way I can have a wild old time without spoiling the 'normalising effects' of the Prozac. I think what most of these medical specialists don't realise is that not everyone wants to be normal, to be saved from depravity. There are certain urges in you from very early on which I suspect are with you until the end, whenever that is.

There is one dream I've had, I keep having: it's about this lane, this walk. I loved it when I was a kid, really a kid. Shamash and I used to go on this walk to David's house in Elizabeth Bay, or Betty Bay as they called it. It was just off Macleay Street, a brick lane that went to all these gorgeous little bridges and gardens with ponds full of fish and stairways that looked too ancient to be in Australia. I used to beg Shamash to let me go to David's on my own but he wouldn't permit it. 'Too close to the Cross for a child,' he'd say. Well, this little walk appears, somewhat differently, in my dreams. It's night and instead of being full of sweet childish things it's chock-full of sex stuff; sexual activities that it's quite difficult for me to negotiate my way past. The thing is, I get quite excited by it but I am trying not to be distracted; I'm on my way somewhere. Then, sometimes my Mum's there too and even though all the other sex is just like men in a beat, she's there and a couple of blokes are giving it to her as well. This doesn't disturb me, but I try to go over 'cos she's waving to me, and then I look in the pond where the fish used to be but they aren't fish any more, they're condoms. I go to reach for one and then I realise they're not condoms but cheesestick wrappers. I start looking for a full one (by full I mean full of cheese not cum) because I'm sure there should be some full ones in there but I never can find one.

Brigitte sighs. 'Oh, Darl, that's sad, that's your childhood you're mourning, that's all the things that are gone.' She's very sentimental, Brigitte, she takes it all mega seriously, deeply, and she's got no time for cynics when it comes to dream interpretation.

'Think about it, Vas, the place where Martin wouldn't let you go on your own, the place where you went anyway, if not literally then metaphorically in terms of the sex. You know what I'm saying, Darl? And the cheesesticks, your Mum, and a life that you have designed mostly around sex, you admit that much yourself. But you know what I think, Vas, what I really think is that if you are invited back into the dream (with Brigitte you have to be 'invited' back into dreams) I think you may very well find a full cheesestick there. This may sound a little kooky to you but if it were me I'd go down to Macleay Street in my waking life, buy a chee-sestick from the corner shop and put it in that pond down there in Elizabeth Bay. It sounds crazy I know but it will help your subconscious mind to know there really is one in there, that your childhood is alive and well inside you, that nothing is ever truly lost forever.'

So I did it. I went into The Mixed Business of Babylon and bought a cheesestick. You'd have to be on Prozac to follow that sort of advice wouldn't you? A grown man putting cheesesticks in a pond in Elizabeth Bay Park. Well I've done worse things than that in parks. With Brigitte I feel I have to do what she says, superstition if you like, but even having done it I get anxious, anxious that when I am invited back into the dream, I will go to that pond with deliberate knowledge and still fail to get the damn cheesestick. It is these types of neuroses that I hope Prozac will help combat. Of course I then worry that the drug itself will repress my 'dream mechanism' so I won't 'receive'; it'll come but I won't be 'taking calls'. Does the brain have a poste restante where later I can claim the 'invitation' I apparently need to go back and reclaim my childhood?

Maybe I just go to Brigitte because she calls me Darl.

Responsibility for one's self. This seems to be my recurring stumbling block; at 20, I seem to be having difficulty reconciling myself to a life spent taking that very responsibility. Perhaps there's a loneliness now that I can't deal with, that burnt-out-ness I was warned about again and again. Maybe it's 'allowed' for me to admit I didn't always know what I was doing, because I didn't. Shamash will forgive me for failing in some ways but we'll always be freaks. It's the love bit that bothers me; I've damaged 'love' somehow, lost its definition, its demarcation lines.

MYSTERY

I haven't been out today. I could use some coffee and I'm out of bread, but some days I can't stand it. I don't feel like 'greeting my public'. There's a woman around the corner in the incredibly overpriced supermarket who calls everyone 'Love' and has the most elaborate 'do' for her hair every day – she's a bit like Mrs Slocombe on that Pommy show. She wears bright purple eye shadow and smokes Holiday 50s.

One of my neuroses is that I can't work out why people are looking at me. I know why they look at her, and believe me, it takes some effort in Darlinghurst to be noticed just for what you look like. I hope when they stare it could be because I'm cute and guys of my age are often admired for that very reason. Oxford Street is surely the Mecca for boy-watching in this town. Sometimes I wonder whether people are watching me because they're homophobes who have come to Oxford

Street just to gawk at the freaks. Then of course there is the other reason, that I'm exactly who I am, that dangerous (former) teenager who made faces at the cameras during one of the decade's biggest legal storms in a teacup.

Brigitte has been nosing around to find me an agent who might sell my story for top dollar. She's talking to a group called Q.U.I.M. (Queer Ultra-Integrity Management). They came up with an immediate offer from *New Weekly* of ten thousand.

'Not enough,' I said. 'God we were in the news plenty. Lindy Chamberlain got more than that.'

I don't know much about these things, not about magazine rights and shit. I'll wait for a better offer. I am, was, news and I want to give them all the secret 'filth' they were hankering for. I want to pull down my 13-year-old's undies and let them see what's there during the forbidden years. I want them to see me confident, clear-skinned at 15, 16; they can see me do all sorts of grown-up stuff at those ages. You see I'm the one who owns me at all those ages. They tried to tell me I didn't back then, but now, at 20, they can't tell me that. Shamash and I have paid and paid for our stolen, not uncomplicated pleasures. It's a user-pays world; I want some of their consumer dollars, I want them to pay for the 'perverse' pleasure we've given them. If it's true as the papers said back then that 'Sydney's Art World Was Rocked To Its Bohemian Foundations' then let's rock it again, let this be a scandalous exposé of those 'paedophile rings' that Shamash supposedly headed.

Lets snare them into the orgies of underage sex that apparently went on in Shadforth Street – 'Choreography For

Kids' as the *Port Jackson Courier* put it. But let them be led and teased slowly, give them almost enough prosaic foreplay to be ready for the literary 'fucking' they're going to get; then just before they're ready fuck'em anyway, without lube or amyl. Get 'em by surprise and fuck'em good I say.

After the Sleaze Ball seduction, Shamash was nervous about being demonstratively affectionate, to say the least. We became a little more distant with each other, and he involved himself with work.

In that last year of primary school I sat the entrance exam for Savant Grammar and passed. For a Bohemian like Shamash, it was a conservative choice, and possibly a little unkind, full of well-bred future bankers and stockbrokers already in an ambitious frenzy to get into the eighties yuppie boom that was going on in the 'real world' outside. Shamash thought I should board. I think our 'incident' had created the need for me to be elsewhere for some of the time.

I guess it gave him more space in his life, too. He was 31 by then, more of a director than a dancer. He was the public face of the company, often being interviewed for arts programs, always going to cocktail parties, charity AIDS dos. He was a typical Sydney socialite in many ways; warm, charismatic, approachable yet secretive, cool, a little flippant and very non-committal. People who knew him socially loved him straight off, but to work with he was apparently difficult, disorganised and a little vague. 'A dizzy North Shore fugitive,' David would say, 'possessed of a capricious artistic temperament.'

Thelly gave him a serve about boarding school too, about sending me to another predominantly male world. I sulked about it, but I went.

What he sought to do when he sent me away (apart from take the heat off himself) was perhaps temper my exploding sexual appetite. Boarding school was not the best place for that. I'm not saying it was an orgy any more than Shadforth Street was, but there were more opportunities where some sort of sexual contact could be engaged in. With my stolen amyl bottle and advanced stage of pubescence, I proved a popular tutor to some of the others in the art of masturbation. The stolen pornography was only ever shown to my 'graduate students'. At boys' schools there are also sure to be one or two masters with a penchant for young fellows. If my advances towards Shamash turned out to be in vain, I could still manage to supplicate a couple of masters, both to my knowledge still at large, still educating the children of paid-up establishment members. I bet they were sweating during the trial, dirty old fuckers.

So there I was, snatched from the heart of Sydney to that dull place, which boasted fresh air, hearty military food and lots of sports. Of course it had a splendid pass rate and really was a 'fine place for young men' – yeah, yeah, yeah. It was old-fashioned and promoted values I know Shamash would have hated – though perhaps he was possessed of a North Shore reactionary streak. In such schools those values are subliminal; you can never put your finger on their wrongness. At Savant it was all about achievement, all about how lucky we were to have the opportunity to be there, how thousands of hungry, capable boys apparently lurked, virtually outside the gates, eager to take our places should we squander our extraordinary opportunity.

That was bullshit. I got in and I wasn't that smart. The school had hopes that I would do things theatrical, as my name suggested, but I didn't show much interest and boys' schools don't particularly encourage interpretive dance unless it's the more violent type on the football field. I hated all those things. Cricket bored me senseless and I could only imagine it being tolerable if matches were played in England next to an ancient church, not next to a Caltex service station in Sydney's north west. You see, if my life were to resemble a Dickens novel, as it does to some extent, I often felt I would like to have risen class wise and found myself once more in the green and pleasant land. For all my grumbling and bitter proletariat background there is a hint of the nouveau riche in me now. England would be a more delightful place to be if one were offering the vicar more tea than it would be offering a pox-ridden wharfie a blow job for 10 quid: ''Ere an' no funny business ni'ver y'ear? Cum in me mouf an' I'll sting ya for anuver fiver.'

It was at Savant that other boys started to give me shit about my Dad being a poof. With the adolescent fascination for reproduction, my origins became a source of the grossest speculation. Travis Cornell was the big bully for a couple of years (until he pushed some little kid off the train, leaving him a paraplegic, and got expelled). He'd heard about fist-fucking somewhere and loved to make up ways in which that activity may have resulted in my conception. A boy on the end of a fist is rather like a glove puppet; hence my nickname. He mastered the fisting gesture as an abusive greeting, the fist turning into a painful punch for me at the end. Cornell used to pin me down and try to fist me. I could tell he loved the idea of this. Even through my trousers he could manage to get two fingers up my arse. Puppet Show became the war cry for this particular playground performance, an event staged weekly, then monthly, then, thankfully, less and less. The first year I was there I went through a dozen pairs of pants. Sometimes both my pairs of trousers would be torn before I could replace them or before Thel could sew them up. I heard a rumour that Cornell got bashed really badly at the beat at Obelisk beach a couple of years back. If only all bashings could be administered with such karmic judiciousness.

When I went home from school on weekends things gradually got better. Shamash started confiding in me again, started letting me back in his room so we could loll about on his bed as we'd always done. But I was getting to be much more 'grown up', my voice quavering from time to time. I didn't tell him about the school brutality; I didn't want him up there making it worse. And I didn't want to embarrass him with the stories the kids told about him. I wanted to revive some toughness from my own childhood. Inside me, Johnny was there accusing me of getting soft, of forgetting what the real world was like, forgetting that what lay inside my torn trousers was of value. It was just ripening and it was gear that could get me things. If I could be handsome, if I could look like some of those boys from Potts En Pointe, I could have whatever I wanted.

Thelly never seemed to be concerned that Shamash and I were so tactile with each other. She never commented except to say she wished her husband had been as good with their kids as Shamash was with me. 'A family is as good as the love that's in it,' she'd say. 'I don't care what you call "a family" but I do know I had to do all the loving in our house. There's plenty of your traditional nuclear families that leave a lot to be desired.' I didn't really know how 'ordinary' fathers were with their sons, but Shamash always said he hoped I would grow up knowing how to cuddle him, a knowledge his father never passed on to him. We had always touched each other, massaged each other, lain around the house together. It was just something beautiful we did, something I treasured. Maybe Grandpa was right to keep his distance, maybe Stoic, Spartan affection as far as dads are concerned is the way to go in order to keep male society at a nervous arm's length from itself. But I loved our cosy calm before the storm.

At school I made friends with Owen, a wiry sort of guy with sandy hair who always wore way oversized jeans and baseball caps when he wasn't in 'Savant Row' (our name for the 'fabulous' designer range launched by our school the year we started). His Dad went to the States all the time and got a different baseball cap each trip. Owen wasn't interested in baseball but was pretty into rap and stuff so he wore them for that. His Dad was really into American sports and constantly tried to foster an interest in his son. Owen was much more interested in the Beastie Boys or L.A. gang warfare, and he seemed disappointed we didn't have crack here yet. Owen was shaping up to be a faggot as well – I think we saw that in each other straight away. He was the first person I told about my Dad being gay, and I guess Owen wasn't as discreet about that disclosure as I hoped. Owen didn't admit he was gay then, I don't suppose I really had either, but he was very interested in my Dad. He was particularly interested in the amyl as well; he was keen on getting wrecked, more keen even than I.

We'd sit in the back of the stables snorting it, not having sex, just giggling, making up these stupid stories about masters masturbating with brooms up their arses or fucking Ms Smedley while she said all this shit in French: '*Ma tante est sur la mer.*' It's not funny now but you piss yourself about that sort of crap at school.

'How big do you reckon Smedley's cunt would be?' Owen would say.

'Oh, about the same size as Mr McCrede's arsehole,' I'd say.

'What would she keep up there?'

'Heaps and heaps of stuff, a portable CD player.'

'Which would be wrecked from all the cunt juice.'

'Oh for sure it'd be wrecked. It'd be fucked I reckon.'

We'd nearly be sick laughing, our heads throbbing, faces flushed from the chemicals. Once we got one of the horses, Mystery, to snort the stuff. She went spastic and kicked a paling out of the stable. We got caught for that but lied about why she did it. The teachers thought we were smoking down there, burning her with a cigarette. They never turned up any cigarettes when they searched my room. They did, however, find a *Hung* magazine.

'Young Vaslav Usher seems to be under some dubious

moral guidance,' I could imagine them saying in the staffroom as they shifted from one foot to another. 'What's the world coming to when kids can find this sort of filth titillating?' I can just see them adjusting their glasses to look at some beautiful blond piece of trash who's sweating cos he's got so much cock crammed up his arse. 'It's just not natural.'

Perhaps rolled up, or even loosely folded, that magazine might have fitted nicely up old McCrede's arsehole.

CHERRY

They say Prozac's not good for creativity, but some days I tend to disagree – besides, there's nothing really new under the sun to say is there? We're just programmed flesh puppets with a limited repertoire of words and responses. Sometimes I say as little as possible. SILENCE = PEACE as well as DEATH.

For example, just as Shamash had all those problems with his mother and acceptance and shit, *Marie Claire*'s mother couldn't care less about her being a lesbian. I know this disappoints her because her mother's always been too busy with her job to pay her the attention she apparently needs. *Marie Claire* puts on all her weird outfits and shows her Mum. Her Mum just shrugs and says, 'If you don't mind looking ridiculous that's up to you – at least I don't have to worry about you getting raped in that gear, you look like some teenage bag lady dragging that stupid Estelle around instead of a shopping jeep.'

'Can you believe that?' *Marie Claire* says to me over the phone. 'Estelle, a fucking shopping jeep, and *rape*. Heaps of really hip girls get raped, raped because breeder scum from the suburbs resent their individuality. She is so self-obsessed, my mother, and so mindlessly suburban. I've had to put up with all her different boyfriends all my life. One of them, I know, would have sexually abused me if he'd had the chance. He came into the bathroom once when I was in the bath then pretended like it was a mistake. *Hullo*. Anyway, I fixed him with a stare like come one step closer and your balls are bubblebath. If the latest one wasn't sooo gross I'd be tempted to seduce him just to teach her a lesson. Do you know what she said to me after the show? The second one, not the first one. Do you know what she said? "I couldn't see that much new in the second show, Allie." She insists on calling me that even though I no longer answer to it. All that genderfuck stuff in the second show just went right over her head. Estelle and I are thinking about just doing women-only shows because the het crowd is so fucked but even in the dyke scene it's not your talent but who you know – or root – that gets your show on. When I get into NIDA they'll be begging for my shows.'

I hold the phone away from my head, noticing how Estelle has dropped out of *Marie Claire*'s future theatrical plans. I wish to myself that NIDA would take her. I don't tell her that the 'genderfuck' in the second show went over my head also, and I have never even lived in the suburbs: 'Well at least your Mum accepts you as a dyke,' I say, hopefully.

'Accepts! Accepts! She doesn't accept shit because she doesn't care – you have to care before you can accept, Vas. God, don't you know anything?'

Apparently not. If she manages to get into NIDA I'll go to UNSW and do Medicine. No I'll do Pharmacology – there's more money in it and more scope for creativity.

Not much happened at Savant about my stolen *Hung* magazine. I was given a punitive assignment to be done on Friday afternoon instead of playing sport, which didn't bother me. The magazine was seized before the nature of the pornography was revealed to any of the other kids, and nothing was reported to 'Dad'. I think the staff were all too aware of Shamash's sexual orientation, of his AIDS involvement and of the probable source of my pornography. The whole situation seemed to be one that they were quite incapable of negotiating. I hadn't even shown the magazine to Owen, but you've got to be very cautious at that age. If my feelings about Owen were wrong, it would have been diabolical to show him, especially as we shared a room. Also, he got to be more like a brother than a sex playmate. We did muck around once or twice but it was more for his benefit than mine. He wanted to see what the 'stuff' looked like when you had a wank, I showed him and he quickly went on to produce his own.

The important thing about that magazine is that although nothing was said at the time, the occurrence was registered then stored somewhere, and it became a nail in the coffin further down the track. But let's dally a little longer on those salad days, jolly boating weather on the Hawkesbury and all that:

'Boys, boys, yes Mr Usher that means you, too. You are a boy, aren't you?'

'Yes sir, I was last time I looked.'

'He was the last time Owen Henley looked too, sir,' added one of my fellow students.

'That's enough of that Bilbury, get those boats cleaned and put away. Usher, see me for a minute when you're back in your uniform.'

It was my 14th birthday. I'd been at Savant for twelve months, almost, and Shamash was going to Amsterdam with the dance company. He wanted to take me as a belated birthday present, which meant my leaving school two weeks before the end of term. Of course it wasn't the sort of interruption Savant usually approved of, but the school 'understood that education had other sides as well, travel being one of them'. Besides, not much happened at the end of term. Wank wank wank. I hate that ponderous seriousness adults have. Like they have so much power, movers and shakers. 'Get a life,' I would have liked to say to those teachers. 'I'm going to Amsterdam, what could be more interesting or important than that?' As if Savant Grammar was Oxford or Cambridge when in fact it was a shit hole with only one building that was a hundred years old, and that had been moved there to give the place character. 'Good-fucking-bye Mr Chips-head.'

I felt very important getting whisked away by Shamash, who arrived looking so cool in his Ray-Bans. 'Well, my darling boy, it's a white Christmas for us this year.

Amsterdam and perhaps Ye Olde England. How about that?'

'I don't care about England. I don't really wanna go there.'

'C'mon Kiddo, we should go there. I want to go back over stuff for myself, too, you know.'

'Shamash, do we have to?'

'What are you scared of?'

'I don't know.'

We were in Hornsby by then. I was feeling better and better the closer we got to Sydney and McDonalds. Truth was I didn't care where we went.

'How many shows in Amsterdam, Shamash?'

'Just three, but I want to go on to London to see about some shows there for next year. If the reviews in the Dutch papers are good, that should clinch it. Mind you, I always get a little nervous in England.'

'Why do you think I don't want to go? Someone's bound to have known Angelique. I'm scared of something weird happening.'

'We'll see how the reviews go. You don't have to come with me to any of my London engagements. David can do that or Ashley.'

'Who's Ashley?'

'This guy I've met whom I like.'

'Is he a dancer?'

'No, a make-up artist, actually.'

'For Potts?'

'He is now. Rachel left in a huff about something so we've put him on. He's good.'

'Was he put on *pre* or *aprés* affair?'

'*Pre*. You'll like him, he's fun. You're not jealous are you, Vas?'

'Nah, you haven't had a boyfriend in ages. Is he young?'

'Twenties.'

'Good looking?'

'Of course, but he's mine you hear.'

'Mirror mirror on the wall. One day, Shamash, the mirror will say, "Shamash yours is beauty true, but beauty more I see afar, imprisoned in Ar-ca-dia."'

'Well Kiddo, all that rowing seems to be doing your arms and chest good. That fabulous pale English skin's lookin' good, too, but I think I've still got a year or two before I have to slip you the poisoned apple. And what's so bad about Savant, that Mr McCrede seemed okay.'

'Doof, my God Shamash, do you realise how daggy and just like a typical parent that sounds? Can't you remember how teachers were always like that to your parents, how they are one way to kids and another to the parents? Don't you ever get like those bourgeois turd-parents other kids have.'

'Bourgeois! So we're using that word now.'

'Yes, and a lot of other words besides, like fuck and cunt. And they're all words I've heard in Shadforth Street. It's just I know what bourgeois means now, and if I keep going to Savant I guess I'll be using it quite a bit.'

'I dare say you will.'

'Will I have my own room in Amsterdam?'

'Well we've got a two-bedroom apartment. It looks quite lavish and tacky in the brochure. But I want you to be nice to Ashley, I want y'all to get along now.'

106

'Yes, Dad.'

I was just so pleased to be out of that shit hole for six weeks I didn't care about anything. I knew I would be spoilt rotten on that trip.

Ashley seemed okay. He mucked around a lot, which was good, and not in that daggy way either like some people do when they're trying to be 'in with the kids'. His was more a 'couldn't give a shit' type attitude, and he had that twinkle in his eye that told me he was BAD. He told me what the mile high club was, and I asked Shamash if they were going to join it on the plane. They both looked askance, sort of smiling. 'Well, we already have,' said Shamash. 'That trip to Perth last month, it was a night flight and boring. Best to do it on those shorter flights. These big ones are a bit too long to be sexy.' Ashley said, 'Oh, I dunno, depends what sort of medication you have for the flight.' Shamash scowled at him with his 'not in front of the child' scowl.

My sexuality was becoming a worry to Shamash. He felt nervous about divulging too much to me and guilty if he didn't include me. With Ashley there it was easier. Ashley had no responsibilities and didn't pretend to have. I could tell he thought it was wild to be going out with someone who had such an unusual family set-up.

The Amsterdam apartment was in Ruysdaelstraat. It was indeed very tacky, with a huge spa bath. Ashley and Shamash joked that it had an 'international gay bath-house style of decor', but I thought it was pretty cool; the mirrors on the bedroom ceiling were the crowning glory.

107

I went sightseeing with Dove, one of the dancers. She and I went to Anne Frank's house, which I really wanted to see. We were both disappointed that only one room was furnished and how it wasn't such a trick concealment after all. Still, my teachers at Savant would be impressed. Dove took me down all these streets where prostitutes worked from inside their own front windows. I thought about my Mum, and how these tarts had it made compared to her.

There were endless sex shops, one displaying a faded photo of a black man with the largest penis ever. I wanted to go into these places, see all these 'things' they supposedly had. 'Wow, this would be great to tell about at school. Can we go in, Dove?'

'You're too young. Besides, what would your father say?'

In one window was a female dummy on a mechanised bicycle. As she peddled she sent a huge black dildo up and down through a hole in her bicycle seat. In and out this thing went, up into her cunt, and she had this ooohlala expression on her face. Dove grimaced: 'I'd hate to go over a bump on a contraption like that.'

The show wasn't going on until 20th December, but there were rehearsals for Shamash to attend. I stayed at the apartment with Ashley when I wasn't sightseeing. He would sit around, smoking joints, letting me have a few drags on the joint because I kept hassling him. With his shoulder-length hair tied back he looked a bit like a surfie, but in a more poofy and manicured way.

'Martin said you're not that keen on Savant or whatever that school's called.'

'It's a shit hole, I can't wait to be finished school.'

'He told me you were pretty eager to grow up fast.'

'What'd he mean by that?' The hairs on the back of my neck began to rise a bit.

'He reckons every way – sexually, the whole bit.'

I felt a flush of betrayal at this, that Shamash had told this still-new boyfriend so much about me but as my anger rose so did a certain amount of relief, a relief that he had perhaps given me the poisoned apple already. Unbeknown to him. Ashley was bad, just as I intuited, and Shamash didn't even realise.

I considered my answer. 'Yeah, he can't keep me out of trouble, poor old Shamash.'

'Well at least there'd be a few choice opportunities at a boarding school.'

'Not as many as you might think, and it's definitely not encouraged.'

'Not like Amsterdam, hey.'

'Not at all like here.'

'I've got this Dutch porn vid if you want to watch it.'

'Cool with me.'

'They're pretty hot some of these Dutch boys.'

He put it on. Even before the credits had finished I had a raging stiffy. I was determined however to be totally seduced. After all, if you can't get someone to do all the work when you're 14, then when can you? At that age I knew there was something pretty serious about sex, whether with someone my own age or with someone older, but at the same time I didn't have a full understanding of what it was I was trading, what I was giving to get.

What I was trading was danger, absolute freshness, odours that are criminal and intoxicating to imbibe, and an irresistible feyness. The last thing more than anything was the lure. For Ashley it was a hunt, a search for truffles; the sexually hungry adolescent somehow fighting the inevitable descent into adult appetites and grown-up depravity. Brigitte says it is the original sin, the ancient fear that as we squirm beneath our first victor, as we give ourselves to the pleasures he offers, we are losing something irrecoverably; we fear it's our soul, but it's not. It's just our innocence.

But back to that moment, when the hobbledehoy is squirming, saying yes without uttering a word, feeling a confident finger pushing inside him. It is the beginning of some sort of ruin, but he knows not what. He knows that whatever the ruin is he's helpless to stop it. The seducer knows that he will 'give', eventually.

'Is that okay? Am I hurting you?'

'No, doesn't hurt.'

'You like it?'

'Yeah.'

'A lot?'

'Yeah, a lot.'

And he's working the hobbledehoy, gently, hotly, and with increasing certainty about the result. But he must be careful. Hobbledehoy is like a kitten or a puppy, squirming, charged with excesses of youthful electricity, smelling like sweet milk but getting dirtier by the minute. He must be nursed, led gently so his mind doesn't change, so he doesn't get a rush of hormones that make him sullen and contrary. The dotard hates that, that would be a failing, a source of guilt and rage. The cherry, still moist in its glorious chamber, the innocence, not yet lost.

I was lying on the gaudy red and black carpet, my dick already pushing into its cheap acrylic pile. Ashley was sitting on the chair with a Heineken in one hand. And I, feeling Ashley's foot ever so gently brushing the inside of my ankle, did what I'd seen Shamash do; ever so slightly, I parted my legs.

'Hot stuff, hey Vas?'

I nodded. He pushed his foot further up my inside leg and I lifted my hips just enough for him to get his foot under the front of my bicycle shorts if he wanted to. He did want to.

The Dutch boys were getting very carried away, fucking without condoms, cumming from various angles in the blurry pastel shades of a European summer afternoon. And wetness was making its way all over the front of my shorts. Ashley sat beside me, his fly already opened (you can't hear buttons being undone). He looked at his dick, reaching to pull my shorts down a little. I was breathing heavily, I just wanted him to do it all, show me all. His looked big next to mine, more threatening perhaps, but also more exciting.

'Which things out of the movie would you like to do, Vas?'

'I dunno, whatever's fine with me.'

'Whatever it is then.' He kissed me, his beery, smoky breath unlocking memories, and a fresh emission surged forth. 'Horny boy.' It was true enough. He lay me back down and pulled off my shorts and jocks in one go. I felt relieved, taken care of. He licked all the wetness from the end of my

111

cock and I groaned. I put on that fey expression, lifted my legs as his tongue went under and between them, flickering gently over my almost hairless virgin arse.

'Is this okay what we're doing Vas? Are you happy about it?'

'Yeah,' I said pushing aside images of Shamash coming back early.

'What about that, then?' he said, glancing down at his own erection.

'You want me to suck it?'

'I wouldn't say no.'

So I did. I lunged onto it. He lay back on the floor with a loud moan while trying to kick his trousers off. I dare say it wasn't the most stylishly performed fellatio, but he had Shamash for that. He wet his finger and gently started to work it into me while I tested how much of his dick I could get into my mouth without gagging.

We broke for a minute, and he went and grabbed some poppers.

'Have you had these? I believe a bottle or two have gone missing.'

I sniffed the bottle, feeling the familiar rush as his finger tickled my now wet arsehole. 'Phew,' he gasped. 'Your Dad was right – you're on fire pretty early buddy.'

My head throbbed. I was feeling stupid from the amyl and carelessly said between gasps of sensation, 'Did he tell you about us?'

'Us? You and him? He hasn't has he? My God!'

The sensation got to me then – the anger, the dope, the sex, the amyl. I felt sick. I had to run to the bathroom.

112

'I don't believe it,' Ashley said, rolling on his back, half laughing, half choking. 'This is too twisted – this is wild.'

ACCOMMODATION

The sickness I felt. The loss of innocence without even having Ashley steal my cherry. I still feel sick about that betrayal, about how right Shamash was in his warnings. Worse still was the danger, the danger in the BADNESS I saw in Ashley. For all my pretensions I was not in his grown-up league as far as games and manipulation were concerned. I thought just the sex itself was the limit of being BAD. How little I knew.

I went to bed shaking and crying, and contemplated my tear-streaked face in the mirrored ceiling. I wondered what would happen. What unimaginable, monstrous demon had I unleashed? Myriad possibilities filed through my mind as the infinite nature of grown-up treachery first dawned on me.

Ashley left me alone that night. He probably thought it was more empowering to him to let me contemplate the horrors. For me to gradually realise how important he could be to me, how 'good' he could be, if I played my cards right. But that night I cried for my Dad, I cried for the childhood I had been so careless with, so eager to discard. I was grief-stricken when I finally flushed innocence down the toilet with the vomit and the toilet paper I'd used to wipe away Ashley's saliva from my bottom, the tiny piece of my anatomy that was soon going to seem like my *raison d'être*.

I knew I'd be needing Johnny real soon. He was winking at me from where he slouched by the garbage dump in the council estate. In my mind's eye he was making lewd gestures just like those trashy boys in the porn movies, his hand outlining the erection in his torn jeans, his other hand fingering his mouth for saliva, for lube. He was mustering his strength, weighing his sex because that's all he had to sell, that was his only ticket out of the council estate and at that stage his only ambition.

I slept finally, fitfully, not knowing what Ashley might say. He said nothing to Shamash, calculating the best uses he could make of my tiny slip. Ashley had work to do for the show, though you would never have thought so the way he lolled about like some expensive porn diva. Spending his time drinking, smoking joints, waxing himself and going off at all hours to the solarium. David secretly called Ashley 'Nancy Spungen'. I don't know whether the others liked him; I got the impression from Dove that she thought he was a creep, but he was 'married' to the director so no one said too much.

There were no further advances from Ashley until after Christmas. Everything was set for the trip to England. I was supposed to fly over with Shamash and David while Ashley waited in Amsterdam, but I got sick. Probably part guilt, part something I ate and part fear of going. Shamash couldn't cancel any of the London engagements; there were some big deals involved. I assured him I'd be fine. Ashley said he'd look after me, feed me chicken soup. He winked at me and I thought, Let the Devil in, *I* am the chicken soup.

My illness vanished as soon as they departed; I guess I was more scared of England than anything else. Ashley seemed to know what I'd done and why. He let the thought of more sex hang in the air, his every move suggesting it; he watched me, touched me, then withdrew. He forced me to go to him for further instruction, my eyes begging him to finish what he'd started.

He and I seemed to have already formed some sort of contract of silence; he wouldn't tell if I didn't. More importantly, he wouldn't mention what I'd said if I played his game. Already I was starting to hate him but I was so excited at the prospect of sex – of him being in a power position over me – that I tried to imagine it as some sort of *Dynasty* set-up. I'd work my butt off to buy his silence, to not have Shamash ever know how I had betrayed him. If I wanted to be a grown-up so much I had to start work right away, in the bedroom, where all grown-ups earn their keep, forge bonds and conflicts. The bed was the performance space of adulthood, the ideal location for an X-rated puppet show. We had nearly six days to play Ashley's game, and what a game that was.

'You're not scared of getting into all this stuff are you, Vas?' he said, as he gently pushed an extra finger into me and rubbed lube down the length of his cock. He'd already tried graduated dildos up there and it seemed that I had finally reached the point of offering him the accommodation he sought.

'If we're going to do it we should use a condom, though.'

'It's alright, I'm clean. I've been tested for AIDS and I'm only doing it like this so you get to start off, at least, with the "real thing". I wouldn't put you at risk any more than your own Dad would. Trust me.' He smiled, one of his department store catalogue smiles, a smile remembered from when he used to model in them. His mention of Shamash hung like cigarette smoke in the air.

How well I'd been educated about safe sex and how easily he got into me without a condom. Of course there were the unspoken things, like 'Shut up freak, you're not in a position to make deals', but it takes maturity to articulate what's going on between those unuttered lines.

'You're going to love this, mate,' he said, as he prepared to enter me, 'but you've got to relax, breathe deeply and very slowly. Then I'll start. We can take as long as we want 'cos the whole idea is that you end up liking it just as much as me.'

Johnny was kept at bay to some extent by Ashley's patience, and I suppose I was lucky to be initiated by someone so considerate. In the days that followed I was transformed from uncertain adolescent to carnal virtuoso.

We had sex two or three times a day in the apartment then rushed about doing other things so we could at least appear to have been usefully employing our time when the others returned. Ashley's desired objectives were met when

I began coming to him, already lubricated; hunger fighting modesty as the child metamorphosed into the freak Shamash had warned me about. Ashley loved the freak he had created. I was channelled by then, my rampant hormones and premature sexual appetite anaesthetising me to the phenomenal guilt I felt about Shamash. I was betraying him in one sense but I hoped saving him in another. I felt wet inside all the time, full of Ashley's cum. How easy and safe for him to have a fresh, undiseased boy–child to download into.

Was I the victim? What about the raw sexual pleasure that accompanied the quite extensive sexual apprenticeship I served those few days in Amsterdam. Am I to retrospectively go back and un-enjoy whatever it was I mistakenly thought was pleasure at the time?

I'm not saying Ashley was right to do what he did, and he revealed himself as being even worse later on. But I did enjoy that sex; I got right into it, stayed into it. Teen sex equalled great sex, at the time. Problem is you have to grow up unless you are a teen suicide.

Shamash must have picked up something of what was going on when he got back. You can't have that much sex without people smelling it or sensing it. Ashley's answer was, 'Martin, how could you say such a thing? I would no more touch the boy than you would in that way.'

Shamash was terrified, of course, but never said anything to me at that stage. I was explosive, contrary and manipulative then. I knew Shamash was praying that we would get through my adolescence without some catastrophic incident; he feared that my behaviour could derail our entire existence. Perhaps he feared me as the enemy despite all the love he had for me, when the real enemy was the man beneath him, snorting amyl as Shamash fucked him, Ashley getting off on sex with Shamash knowing that in the next room lay the son he'd been giving it to the day before. What could Shamash have done had he known his own boyfriend was cheating on him with me? He might have guessed that I probably had not been unresponsive to the advances made, he didn't know what I had said, the extent of my revelation about our encounter. I know what I would have done – I would have said 'This is not happening.' What else could he do without opening gaol gates and institution doors, and with every other conceivable type of hell breaking loose?

The race for me to get to 18 was on. And I didn't mind returning to Savant for the time being. At least I could pick on someone my own size.

SEX
DWARF

So it was *ciao* to Amsterdam and all its canals, goodbye to innocence and modesty and hello to Vas the monster, abuzz with hormones, desire and guilt. Real guilt for the first time in my life. A new Vas with a glint in his eye. The sort of 14-year-old boy who frightens men in the changing room at the pool, frightens them with undeniable sexuality, self-possession and erections that make it indecent to shed Speedos in the shower. A boy who scares them with the knowledge that they just might put themselves in a situation that could land them in prison, that could wreck the safety of their otherwise decent lives.

We took a train trip to Paris via Austria and spent a few days there. Ashley and Shamash seemed to be going at it a fair bit in the bedroom of the apartment, as if Ashley had to make up for what they'd missed out on while Shamash had been away from Amsterdam. We were right in Le Marais, and

I went walking on my own when the bedroom door shut. I'd had more than enough sex to quieten me down but I still felt aroused by the sound of them, doing heavier stuff than what the hobbledehoy was ready for yet.

We flew back to Sydney, and I discovered that Ashley had already moved in with Shamash before we went to Amsterdam, which I thought was a sneaky thing for Shamash to do without consulting me. What had started out as a temporary arrangement had turned sort of permanent, and I couldn't go into Shamash's bedroom like I used to. When Ashley had the chance to fuck me he did it in my room. He said it was kind of cute on a single bed. My appetite was such that I wasn't too concerned where it happened, and my guilt was adequately suppressed by hormones and desire. It was after, and between times, that I felt the distance grow between Shamash and me. I didn't really want to do it with Ashley anymore, but my libido was such that I seemed unable to say no.

Late one Saturday afternoon Ashley was fucking me in my room when Thel came to Shadforth Street to drop something off; she wasn't usually there on weekends. Thel was not keen on Ashley, you could tell. He was all over her like they were ancient friends, which wasn't Thelly's style, but anyone could tell she hated him grabbing her. She tried to be civil and he tried to pretend he was part of the furniture. Ashley got his trousers on in time and headed out the door; I only had shorts to pull back on. Her eyes narrowed when he sauntered out of my room.

'What are you doing in there?'

'Helping Vas with his homework.'

'I can't imagine what you'd be able to help him with.'

'Well pardon me Thelma, you coach him and you're just the help. I'm sure I can shed a little light on an Anne Tyler novel he's read – and can't understand.'

'He's reading *Tales of the City* at the moment.'

My heart was thumping like you wouldn't believe. I was so scared of Thelly finding out. She called me, and I came out trying to look like I had been reading and had not heard a thing. She asked me what book I was reading. I held up *Tales of the City* and she glared at Ashley. He looked up and said, 'What's that report you're writing for school?' '*Dinner at the Homesick Restaurant,*' I said as a gesture to him. I thought, I'll bail him out this time, because I would be ashamed for Thel to know.

She looked flustered for a second, then turned to Ashley and said, 'You just stay out of his room, you hear?'

Ashley said, 'Yes *Mum,*' and did one of his vile facial expressions. No sooner had she gone than he was bouncing back up the stairs saying, 'Where were we? Ah yes, the cumming part, my favourite bit.'

'Not now Ashley. I don't feel like it anymore.' That's one thing about being fucked, you've got to feel like it. This was the first time I'd held out on him – I felt strangely elated about that.

Thelma must have said something to Shamash because he made sure he didn't leave Ashley alone with me after that. They were starting to niggle at each other a bit, and I guessed that other things were going on. Late at night they would come home with an occasional third party. Perhaps Shamash thought if they got into other weird stuff the pressure would be off me. Youth as fresh as mine was, is, a special attraction all of its own, exciting enough just for its decadence and illegality to not require handcuffs, dildos or any of the other assorted accessories that become standard distractions in the drawers of an increasingly jaded homosexual male's boudoir.

Back at Savant Owen and I shared a reasonably normal year 8. We talked filth all the time, farted and did all those healthy boy things. I didn't confide in him about my 'summer adventures' but I did start eyeing off a particular teacher whose gaze tended to linger too long on boys in the change room. I studied the way he fidgeted from time to time, the proximity he seemed to like having with some boys. I became one of those boys.

I didn't move my arm away from him when he leaned close to me over a prac assignment. I made it clear I wasn't going to move away from him at all. I didn't fancy him that much; he was over 30 and balding a little, though his body was in good shape. The excitement was in the thrill, the danger. A danger far greater for him than for me.

I'd learned a new frequency of communication from Ashley. I was suddenly aware that if I looked someone in the eye a certain way and they returned that look, there was no mistaking what it was about. It was an exciting discovery to be able to convey adult depravity through my teenage eyes, to meet my 'superiors' with a gaze that eliminated the years separating us. To at once be an adult alongside them with a shared agenda and the question, 'Do you dare?'

Sir was keen to play the game. It took him months of exchanging those glances before he suggested I stay back to work on an assignment I was having problems with. Thanks to this incident, I achieved a pass for the next two terms at least.

He was more nervous than I when push came to shove, which irritated me a little. Hobbledehoys can start to get a little cocky once they think they've got some power. So after he'd played the standing too close game, the accidental rubbing game, and finally the game was given away by the bulge in his trousers, we went into the prep lab where he, with far less coolness than Ashley, got all hot and clumsy and knelt before my prick.

He sucked it while he pulled his own stiff, but disappointingly small, dick. I asked him if he did other stuff as well. He looked up from the object of his study, and with a perplexed and ridiculous expression on his face proceeded to ejaculate on the floor. I was sort of disgusted at him by that stage; he was so unsophisticated. I quickly zipped myself into my trousers and left him nearly prostrate on the floor. He looked pathetic, and suddenly I felt incredibly powerful. I hadn't cum and I could tell that he would soon be going into a state of near catatonic fear. I smiled to myself at how inadequate grown-ups could be, how immoral and worthless. I laughed at Savant, with all its bullshit about reputation, employing a man like that who could be hoodwinked into criminal activity by a 14-year-old and live in constant fear. A repulsive dotard – subservient to *me*.

I had wanted him to perform well if he was going to do it; I wanted him to control me in some patriarchal way but he wasn't up to it. It wasn't Vaslav who left him in the prep lab of the science room. It was Johnny. Johnny expected better than that. Johnny didn't suffer fools lightly. If there's such a thing as a moral-free playground where pleasure's to be taken without consequence, then he wants a man with the guts to take his pleasure as he finds it. He's got no time for bourgeois fretting and nervy safety checks.

Owen and I were considered sort of cool that year despite us 'possibly' being faggots. The coolness came from the fact that I would steal small amounts of grass from Shamash and roll joints – not very strong ones – to sell for 10 or 15 dollars each. Neither of us needed the money, but we loved the power and reverence we obtained through doing it. We quickly found ourselves surrounded by boys who were destined to be the 'bad ones' when they grew up. Those invited could come to our room and listen to Stone Roses or Depeche Mode if I was in charge or Beastie Boys and the soundtrack to *Colors* if Owen was. He had a portable CD player his Dad had got him in Japan and we hooked it up to the ghetto-blaster we had in there. CDs were still pretty new then, and that *Colors* soundtrack had us all using the phrase 'move over to the side of the road asshole'. We used it as a code for calling someone an asshole:

'Did you go and see Mr Greenland about your late history assignment Usher?'

'No Sir. He's moved over to the side of the road.'

The whole class would go ballistic with laughter and the masters could only wonder what brand of neo-speak they were being excluded from that year.

In Paddington Shamash's love affair had soured. Ashley had been living there for nine months and he fancied that he was entitled to some sort of financial settlement. He'd done pretty well, picking up a 14-year-old's cherry, which surely you don't do every year of your life, and living in the lap of luxury with a beautiful lover. All this because he could do some fancy work with eyeliner and grease paint.

Shamash had retreated into a textbook-Dad niceness with me, telling me on the phone about the break-up as if he were a mother telling a child that 'Mum and Dad need some time apart, to sort things out'. I tried to hide my joy at their separation, not wanting to look like I was scheming in any way. However trashy I may have been, Ashley was the living end. He got 25,000 dollars out of Shamash. I never knew the exact extent of the blackmail, but if it was paid for 'silence' Shamash never got his end of the bargain. Ashley gossiped, he played Chinese whispers – Sydney whispers is probably a better name for it. He told people that the relationship failed because 'Martin's more interested in his own produce – if you know what I mean', and 'How can a jaded old queen like me at 26 compete with a 14-year-old for youth or 'tightness'? He created a whirlwind of rumours then vanished to New Zealand where he worked for some television station, I think. By the time we were in trouble, he was nowhere to be found.

Sometimes I wonder about all this new age crap, about people telling themselves that they're beautiful loving people, trying to harness within themselves some fucking inner angel, goddess, hero or wolf that a book told them they had. Instead, why don't they just allow themselves to acknowledge that really they are deeply corrupted, hopelessly flawed pieces of cosmic space junk. Not that you can't love junk, but what if 'God' just made you that way? Made you a porn star or a junkie. And maybe he made you that way because he likes to watch you being those things. You might enjoy being those things yourself from time to time.

Once on the council estate the kids got a dog to drink some lager. We all laughed like crazy when the dog got pissed and staggered all over the place. We stopped laughing when it wandered out onto the road then got itself skittled. It just lay there twitching and yelping because its back was broken. No one had the money for a vet so it had to be clubbed to death by some kid's brute of a brother. He bashed it and bashed it with a cricket bat, glad of the excuse for some compassionate violence. 'Die you fuck, die!' he shouted. It didn't seem to want to. The boy it belonged to screamed like his throat was cut while his mother cursed us to hell from the landing, told us we were evil, while looking at me the whole time.

Perhaps we're all like that dog, lurching about until we wander out onto the road and get hit by a bus or something. Maybe 'God' finds it endearing or empowering to see his kids blundering about all flesh and blood and guts – each one a divine little fiasco floundering at happenstance's beck and call.

Brigitte says I see everything in such a bleak way. She says there are dark angels, too: 'They count for just as much – life would be pretty damn dull without its darker side. For sins and allegories to be catalogued, illustrated and contextualised they must be perpetrated by someone and I hardly think the creator would be so churlish as to not allow his/her perpetrators a flicker of completion or enlightenment as they feel the impact of that speeding bus or the twilight consciousness of a fatal heroin overdose.'

Brigitte has a car so she doesn't know there's no such thing as a speeding bus on Oxford Street.

This week I'm trying to have a 'proper Brigitte week'. That means following as much of her advice as possible. I've stayed off Prozac and had no other drugs, either. I'm trying to stay away from the dance clubs and sleaze shops that are distracting and sapping me of my energy. I've got to get out of dead-end behaviour, of blameless, aimless wandering. I'm nearing the end of an age where I can continue to just kill time the way adolescents do in their bored despondent way. And I am aware that a lot of my more seedy behaviour is the ultimate inheritance of gays considerably older than myself.

Brigitte says, 'You'll leave yourself nothing to explore when you really are old and depraved. You're not a prisoner of any particular type of behaviour you know, you don't look older than 20 but you worry all the time that you do, don't you?'

She's right about that. She came around, suggested that instead of sitting cramped in my lounge room with all my books (and mess), we go out and have lunch in the sun in Oxford Street – the Paddington end.

'But people might see us,' I laugh.

'Well you don't seem to mind people seeing you at night, and they get to see a good deal more of you than anyone's going to see today.'

I sniggered. She's too much sometimes, Brigitte. 'Why not Victoria Street, or Roy's? It's more groovy and I might see a cute German or French backpacker.'

Brigitte finally dragged me out into that gorgeous sunny day. I was getting a bit pissed on wine as we sat at a table out the front of Roy's. I'd drunk three glasses to Brigitte's one. I felt like I was getting sunburnt, but she said it was wine-burnt. Brigitte was eating her vegetarian Pad Thai while I toyed with some potato wedges that were all crusty with that MSG shit they put on them. She was going off about the hidden talismans in dreams and karmic reflux or some other thing of hers. I was thinking about Kylie Minogue's latest hairstyle and about how I'll never get a six-pack stomach if I keep eating food that's full of fat. I was looking at myself in the reflection from the window, wondering if the creases of shirt across my stomach could be mistaken for a paunch. I was trying to catch my reflection by surprise – you know, see if I could see myself like I was someone else.

I decided that with my hair like it is, bleached and cropped, and with my tight black T, skin-tight F.A. dacks, Italian boots and trashy ultra-silver sunnies, that I did actually cut a pretty damn sexy image. I'm sure the wine helped me to start feeling so positive, but it was a good feeling. I suddenly felt like I was this ageing movie star but kind of still in my prime at the same time. Anyone who recognised me would think, Wow, Vas looks like sex. He's hot, he's a survivor.

Brigitte's probably right when she says I'm paranoid, but when your whole reputation is based on sex, well you can't help feeling like you've got to look desirable all the time. I've got to look like I'm worth going to prison for. Stupid really, but I'd hate people to go off gossiping and saying 'I saw that Vaslav Usher in Victoria Street today and he looked seriously wasted, he's so sad.' That's why sometimes it's better to think about Kylie or Madonna. Both, I tend to think, look better as brunettes.

So while I'm crapping on inside my head like that what should startle me back into the real world but the trundling sound of some sort of trolley.

'What on earth ——?' said Brigitte peering past me. I looked over my shoulder only to see Estelle heading towards us on roller blades with a child's little red wagon in tow. I could see three supermarket bags on the back and a puppy or dog with one of those circus collars that looks like a tutu. She was out of control and the dog was yapping at every person they passed. I was just preparing to ignore her, hoping she wouldn't see me when she passed by, but it was too late.

'Help, Vaslav!' she cried.

Before I could do anything she'd reached out and grabbed hold of a No Standing sign and managed to stop. The problem was she'd picked up so much momentum that the red wagon swung over towards the gutter and ran side-long into a red BMW that was parked there. The dog's yelping partially obscured the sound of the paint being scratched off the car, but there was no hiding the scratch itself.

Estelle looked around. 'Help me!' she hissed through clenched teeth. Brigitte was pretending to read the menu even though I knew she didn't want anything else. The dog had got out of the wagon and was taking a shit under the next table and one of the grocery bags had split, revealing five frozen TV dinners and nine rolls of unbleached toilet paper. Estelle was squatting on her roller blades looking at the scratch on the car while simultaneously trying to obscure it from view. Even Estelle knew a car like that would belong to some rich cunt. Brigitte whispered across the table to me 'What's the bet that car belongs to some Double Bay estate agent or a crime boss.' I thought the red was more in keeping with an estate agent.

I watched Estelle, thinking, She truly is mad. She'd crouched down to fossick through her backpack for lipsticks. She had three in her hand and I couldn't work out what she was doing, then I realised she was matching them up with the paint on the car. She decided on a pinky-red one, which didn't quite work.

'There's nothing I can do Estelle,' I said to her.

'Well you could fucking well save *Marie Claire*'s dinner for a start.'

I looked over at the wagon and could see the dog already starting to tear open one of the TV dinners. I was really annoyed with her but I went and sealed up the bag anyway. Brigitte looked at the dinners and said, 'You don't want to be buying those things, Darl. They cost a fortune, especially at Delphine's Del' Dell.'

Estelle clenched her teeth and looked at Brigitte. 'They are the only things I can get *Marie Claire* to eat while she's sick, as if it's any of your business.' Brigitte looked away, she can't stand hostility and lets it wash over her without ever taking it to heart. '*Marie Claire*'s sick and we're supposed to do a show tonight. That's why I've got Zsa Zsa with me and the only thing she can do is shit and piss.'

'Where did you get her from?' I asked.

'Some stupid trannie in Surry Hills let us rent her for 25 dollars but she can't do any of the things she's supposed to so I'm taking her and her fuckin' wagon back for a refund.'

Estelle and *Marie Claire* are both would-be performance artists in search of funding. At the moment they are pretending to be dykes in the hope of getting a development grant from the Sydney Gay & Lesbian Mardi Gras for a piece entitled 'Kiss Me Pink Lips and Milk Me Like a Cow'. *Marie Claire* is a lesbian but Estelle isn't. I've promised not to tell anyone in case it affects their submission.

Estelle scribbled something on one of the cafe's free postcards in purple Texta. 'I will leave this under the windscreen wiper for the person who owns the car – best to do the right thing,' she said, wrinkling up her nose. I was in shock that she'd ever do the right thing. Perhaps *Marie Claire* is the evil one.

Finally, she gathered up everything and headed off on her calamitous way. I was amazed the dog even got on board the wagon, but it only did because Estelle stole two chips from my plate and put them in there along with the ashtray from our table.

'I don't know what you see in those girls.'

'Neither do I half the time Brigitte.'

As we left I grabbed the note:

Sorry to trouble you
Mr B.M.W.
You've got a scratch
But I've got a snatch

I put it back and looked at the smears of lipstick on the side
of the car. I sniggered. Fancy me thinking she would ever do
'the right thing'.

C O L T

It would have been the Christmas after my 15th birthday. I felt really grown up when I was 15; I was getting confident about the shape of my body. I was much more confident than I am now and I couldn't say I've really slipped into decay just yet. It was all the rowing up at Shitsville Savant. I guess I was toughening up physically and emotionally.

I sort of languished like a porn star in Paddington. I felt I'd pulled something off (no pun intended). Shamash started calling me 'the prince'.

'Is Vaslav the prince going to join Dad and Dave for breaky or is some nymph going to come and feed him peeled grapes?'

'I don't want to go down there and fight for one of those stupid milk crates to sit on while some bloody dog eats my focaccia.'

'One dog, one time, got one-quarter of your toasted sandwich. I thought you liked going out for breakfast?'

'It's just a lot of pretentious old wankers down there.'

David took over. 'So Vaslav is now charging Sydney's supposedly beautiful people with being not only wankers but, horror of horrors, *old*.'

Shamash laughed. 'Leave him. He's been at that boarding school so long he doesn't even realise "old" has been deleted from the Eastern suburbs vocabulary. *We are not old* you vile ingrate. Time shall soon plant its hideous blooms on your fair skin, Sonny Jim.'

'Why don't you two just go, for fuck's sake.'

'Such language in our sacred home, Vas,' said Shamash as they slammed the door behind them.

I studied the angles from which I lay on the couch while I ate crisps or bowls of cereal. That always turned Shamash's friends' heads that did. I was a distraction to guests, and I liked it. The irresistible image of a pumped-up adolescent eating a bowl of cereal, food for food's sake, the hunger of a nubile man. Hobbledehoy no longer.

Moody though, perhaps also a studied mannerism. I'd be lying there watching D-Gen or some shit, going ballistic with laughter. Talking to Owen on the phone. We'd do impersonations in mental voices. But I was always eyeing off the people Shamash had around for one reason or another and they all kept their distance. I was still a kid in their eyes.

After they got back from breakfast that day David went home and Shamash and I were left alone.

135

'I haven't had a hug for the longest time. I miss my boy, you know.' It must have been then he asked me, did I want to talk about Ashley; about what had gone on. I sort of resisted at first, denied anything really happened, but in the end he got serious.

'This is not some trivial urbane little thing we're talking about here. It's getting worse and a bloody sight more complicated as time goes on. I am to blame every bit as much as you, more than you in any legal sense, but for God's sake talk to me. I can't think how anything could be better if you didn't go to boarding school. I don't know whether you're punishing me for making you keep all those secrets. I know it has been difficult, but we haven't done too badly have we? I've given you as much as I can Vas. What would make you happy, Kiddo? I don't know.'

I started to cry then. Really cry. You know what it's like when you try to say stuff when you're crying, you can hardly say the words and then they come out feeling like they've come from another dimension inside you. It's like when you're a baby. I tried to say, 'I'm so sorry Shamash. I was so bad and I know how I hurt you and I don't know how I could hurt you, the only person in the world I love. I'm probably just bad, really bad inside like Mum.' I would have gone on but he came and hugged me and rocked me like I was a baby. I cried and cried while he just kept rocking me. His eyes had tears too but he was stronger. He had a stern look on his face; he had suffered himself. If a heap of bad things happen to you in a row, you can't give them all the same number of tears.

In the end I quietened down to sobs, and he said, 'You

shouldn't say your Mum was bad, Hon. She got you to me, she passed you from one pair of arms to another. That's not bad in this rough and ready world. Tell me what happened. It started in Amsterdam, I know that, so please tell the truth, Vas. Just do me that honour will you?'

So I did tell him everything, almost everything. He told me that it wasn't my fault, blah blah blah, but of course at that age you don't like 'I told you so'. You want things to be your fault but can't cope when they are. I couldn't bear to think I'd fallen into the scenario he'd already warned me about, so I started to be cool about it. Talk man to man, Johnny to Martin:

'Ashley was a cunt, Shamash. I'm not saying that he wasn't sexy – in some ways, he was.'

'Perhaps cunt is the wrong word. Arsehole would be more appropriate.'

'For you perhaps he was an arsehole, to me he was a prick. I was the arsehole. How could you get sucked in by someone like him?' I asked Shamash, as if I were somehow more knowledgeable about these things. 'You could have got something better.'

'If one more person says that to me I'm going to scream. I didn't get someone "better", and don't I know it now. But I'm not perfect, I make big mistakes, too. You want me to have some clean-looking doctor or solicitor like the ones they always seem to have in those American films – the Ken doll in *Parting Glances* perhaps? Life's not like that, Vas. I didn't think he'd try it on with you, or I at least thought there'd be a little warning if he did. I can't be everywhere at once and perhaps I needed to see how predatory you might be getting. I never asked him what he did to – with – you. Do you want to tell?'

'He did pretty much everything. But Shamash, one thing, he never used a condom on me, and I never fucked him, either.'

Shamash started crying then, kind of weeping. He had this sort of gutted, horrified look on his face.

'Ashley said he'd been tested and everything.'

This was difficult for Shamash because he didn't want me to worry unnecessarily about being HIV positive, but he didn't want to sanction or underplay the diabolicalness of what I'd done, either. 'You must never let anyone do that to you! Jesus, Vas, have I not got that message across in the last five years?'

'I bet you did it without condoms sometimes.'

'That's not the point, or it shouldn't be.'

'Well it makes me feel better if you did. That shits me about all these gays – they're not even honest with themselves. I don't think I had much choice in the matter anyway, he kind of tricked me 'cos I said something about you and me.'

'How do you feel now about it?'

I was a teenager so my stock answer to that was a shrug and, 'I dunno.' I suppose I didn't know.

Shamash seemed older that day. Crying does that, but there was something else, too. The worry and the fear. And he was right to be afraid, not of Vaslav his darling boy who would love him 'til he died, but of Johnny whom he hadn't even come face to face with yet. Johnny already knew from which positions he could be best penetrated. He was already sticking things into himself for want of the real thing, he was getting past farting with the other boys and he was already over embarrassment in the change rooms. He was body obsessed, doing stuff to himself for hours in front of the mirror, chafing at the bit for more of the 'real action'. He'd been left in the lurch too. There were Shamash and me sitting together like sex junkies going cold turkey. Father and son, boy and man, both loving and needing each other, and he with his maturity and knowledge was justifiably more scared than me.

He decided that I should go for a blood test just to make sure everything was okay. I said I didn't want to, but eventually we agreed. Our doctor, Andrew, was a friend of Shamash's, but even so, we had to make up a story. We didn't want to have anything more to do with Ashley, and Shamash wasn't sure how Andrew would deal with the truth. Instead we concocted a tale about me and another boy at school who had done 'it', properly, but with no condom. I could hear Andrew saying to Shamash, 'Look, they're 15, it's their first time. Do you really want to worry him about it now? I can't believe he told you he'd done it. Gay kids are usually just as closed with gay parents as straight kids.'

Andrew saw me on his own and asked me a few questions. He was talking about 'the fuck' as if it were only almost a fuck. I said, 'Look, we did the business, he came in there and I shat it out. That was it.'

'Was there much to shit out?' he asked in a medical sort of way.

'Nah, it's no big deal. Dad made me come here.' I was trying to sound worldly about it all.

'Well I don't think I need to lecture you on the safe sex bit. Your father's a champion of the cause and I'm sure you'll be fine, but you do have to wait two weeks before we know for sure.'

I did get nervous those two weeks, but the test was negative and it had been months since my last rendezvous with Ashley. What did show up though, and it was of no great medical concern, was cytomeglovirus, which is harmless enough but is not usually found in a young, sexually naive schoolboy doing it for the first time with a similarly naive chum. Its record on my medical card was another drop of mercury in the barometer of our demise. Fair was changing to stormy.

If I'd stayed on the council estate would anyone have made a national hullabaloo over my cheap honour? I would have been raking in the rent without a second thought about how fragile I was, how tender and young. Mum never had anyone there for her when she began her downward spiral. Poor Mum, what a ghastly life she had. If I hadn't been removed I wouldn't have even thought it ghastly, just ordinary. Most people's lives are shit I reckon but the richer we are the more entitled we think we are to having a code of protection around us. The problem is sometimes the rich are trapped by the very same nets they cast.

Shamash spent years working for AIDS groups, rolling up his sleeves and putting together benefits that cost him money. Then because of my 'complicated' childhood all that was as nothing. Forget the false memory syndrome crap; I remember everything. Move over Laura Palmer, you're not the only one who ever led a double life.

In Paddington I could sneak out at night if I wanted to. Shamash would have been horrified if he'd known I was wandering around Taylor Square some nights. I had to be careful, too. Plenty of people could have identified me. Mostly though, at 3 in the morning they were desperados, junkies, drunks and hookers. I was intoxicated just at being out. I didn't need anything, not at the start. It must have been just before I went back to school when I met this guy only a year or two older than me. Colt, he called himself – a roughish kind of dude from the western suburbs. He was good looking in a slutty, peroxide way and I got sort of addicted to him. He was a prostitute and he'd show off to me how he picked guys up along the Wall: the swagger, indifference and confidence as he sauntered over to a car that had slowed. He showed me how to catch your face in the lights in a way that makes you immediately desirable.

'Always say you're 18,' he said, as if I were 'in training'. I guess I pretended I was. He thought I sounded posh. 'Haven't you got rich folks you can nick some money from dude? Better than having these cunts ramming in and out o' you all fuckin' night. Fuck 'em and rob the cunts I say, or do trick sex – make 'em wanna get rid of ya as soon as they get you back to their place. I'm gunna get enough money together to go up to Surfers. I reckon its full of Jap cunts up there. Don't much fancy havin' fuckin' slap heads rootin' me all night but they have loads o' cash and little dicks. Ya just

141

lie on the beach and enjoy the sun and the drugs. That's what I wanna do.'

Colt excited me because he was like Johnny. I found it hard to imagine that the Japanese would have lined up to have a turn at 'sticking it to him' but I was fascinated by the naivete of his dream. I really wanted to have sex with him but he didn't seem to pick that up; I suppose sex was probably the last thing he wanted to do. I was turned on by the fact that he had had so much sex already. I wanted to put my finger or mouth where so many worthless others had been, that was my fantasy. I imagined that after being fucked by all those tricks he'd be grateful if I offered him the opportunity to fuck me. I thought it would be really romantic and cool in a totally grungy sort of way.

But my subtle advances went largely unnoticed. It became apparent that the way for me to 'get wiv' him' would be to do a trick, a threesome with some punter. So I did one night. I was scared when we got into that Commodore, but Colt had a knife and he seemed to know what he was doing. I worried about my inexperience; I felt green and a little shy about sex for cash, about doing it with someone I'd never seen before. I didn't realise that was the whole point, that was my value, that is exactly what they want – still fey enough to squirm, so young that no lighting could reveal decay; perfect, almost ripe, a delicacy. Exquisite human contraband. I'm ready for my close-up, Mr De Mille.

The threesome was an eye-opener. We snuck into the Hyde Park Plaza and went with this old guy in his 40s up to his suite on the eighth floor. He wanted me and Colt to get off together. This pleased me no end; I was going to finally have a crack at Colt. We had to follow his directions, like 'You start kissing him now and you're getting hornier now so you lie on the bed, now you undo his fly, now you suck his cock', and on it went. He was choreographing a sexual scenario which he only wanted to watch. I was getting quite into it. I tried to ignore the old guy masturbating while he watched us and I could tell with Colt that he wasn't nearly as excited by me as I was by him. For him it was more like mundane work, like going to the toilet, remembering where you left your keys or fixing a household appliance.

While all this was going on, the old guy started taking photographs. This seemed to irritate Colt but it encouraged me to do some of the faces I'd liked in mags. I never thought for a minute about them being developed. I had no sense of them having any consequence. The old guy was saying to Colt, 'Now I want you to fuck the little fella. He's got a tight, hungry little arse which wants fucking, so you fuck him good now.' Colt put on a condom and without ever really looking at me, he fucked me. It hurt a bit more than it had with Ashley, mainly because I was under-lubed and the whole thing was taking place at such a fast pace. The old guy gave me some amyl and I was able to at least imagine that Colt was enjoying it. He made noises as if he was cumming but he never did. The old dude sort of groaned, came and rushed into the bathroom.

As soon as he was in there Colt got the film out of the camera and hid it in his pocket. 'That cunt's not gunna get any souvenirs for his money.'

Colt gave me 40 of the 80 dollars he had negotiated with the old dude and we left. I never saw Colt again after that night. Perhaps he went to Surfers. I don't know, but I saw those pictures a couple of years later. I don't know where the prosecution got them from and they were dismissed as evidence, theoretically, but they got into other hands. One thing's for sure, the media didn't dismiss them as evidence.

'Who, we ask, was holding the camera that took these pictures?' said that ponce in the courtroom as Shamash looked at me across the room with an expression of such grief and confusion that it still features in my worst dreams. Those pics were said to be evidence of the child pornography racket Shamash was rumoured to be running. I don't doubt that Colt would have sold them for a price. He may have seen me in the paper – or on the telly more likely.

I could be Johnny at night, on the beat, and still be Vas in his teen-retreat at Shadforth Street, in the kitchen talking to Thelly:

'Does Dianne like it at Sydney Uni, Thel?'

'Yes, she does and she managed to get in there just fine from a state school. I don't know why Martin thinks he has to send you off to that fancy joint when there's a perfectly good school in Woollahra, which is free.'

'Thelly should you be so outspoken about your employer?'

'Employer indeed. How would he run this house without me? Besides I've said as much to his face. Remember, I've brought up two of my own kids, and Jack was never any help even when he was there. In fact it was like having three kids when he came home sozzled. Dianne wants to move out into some shared house in the inner-west and I guess I'll be on my own then.'

'It's a big house just for you.'

'I know. I'd like to sell it and move up to the mountains, but it is too far to come down here. Homebush is enough of a drive for me, especially at night. At least you're big enough and ugly enough to look after yourself.'

'I'm not ugly."

'That's half your problem. If you weren't so damn full of yourself you might not be such a handful for the rest of us.' She always used to pass me some of whatever she was cutting up in the kitchen – usually a bit of ham or cheese. This time she handed me the neck out of a chicken.

'Yuck,' I said.

'I used to make soup out of those when I was young. We never used to waste anything in those days. Now everyone just buys breasts or throws the rest away. When I started working in Paddington you could hear birds, now all you hear is car alarms and those phones people are starting to get. It all changes so fast; what have people got to say now that can't wait I wonder? Dianne wants one and she's still a student. I'm happy for her to get one when they get cheaper, I won't worry so much when she's out at night . . .'

I thought about my own night adventures. If Thel only knew.

'I 'spose Martin pays you too much to give up this job.'

'You are an impertinent little brat, Vaslav, but you're right. Anyway, are you going to cook the pots of bolognaise that keep you two alive? Neither of you eat enough vegies when I'm not here. You should learn to cook. I'll be 55 next birthday, I should think about retirement one day.'

'You could write a book on the things you've seen in Shadforth Street.'

'There'd be a book in that all right, but I don't think Martin would be too pleased. And I don't think I've got the vocabulary for some of the things. I'd be like one of those royal family servants coming out with the dirt and getting a million dollars for it.'

'Well you'd have two queens to write about, three if you include the brat.'

That was the day I actually confessed to Thel I was gay. She paused for a while and went on stuffing the chicken for dinner.

If Thelly ever wondered about what might have been going on she chose to turn a blind eye. She certainly didn't approve of everything but she wasn't a prude. She displayed the same degree of displeasure to whites being washed with coloureds as she did to David's tales of threesomes.

'David Bergdorf, I've lead the life of a nun for years now and I do not need to be subjected to the sordid details of your life. Tell me about a big win on the pokies or a 200,000-dollar trifecta if you want my pulse to race.' She never liked Ashley: 'Don't get me started on him. The day that one left was the best bit of cleaning this house has ever had. He never lifted a finger around this house and he walked away with more money in nine months than I get in two years. I'm in the wrong business or I'm the wrong sex.'

'Or you're too old.' She looked daggers at me, pointing the knife as she did. I hadn't realised what I was saying and I looked away.

'You said it Vas, not me.'

I can still feel the blush I felt that time. So shameless and so ashamed.

I went back to Savant for year 9. Owen was still rooming with me and he was getting more into bands like 'The Cult'. These days he's a real Seattle boy, too macho in his taste to be the poof he is. I saw him a couple of nights ago at the Shift. He hates any of that 'queenie dance shit'; moshing however hasn't become quite the dance style in gay clubs that he would like. 'Find yourself a grungy little Courtney,' I said. 'Marry the bitch, conceive a gutter child while you're both on smack and that would be well cool.'

'Yeah, make sure she's really twisted, too, hey Vas. Stick all different stuff up her man, yeah? Like Courtney does with stilettos. 'Hey baby, you're too fucking out of it to stop me sticking this beer bottle to you aren't you and she'd say fuck off and I'd say fuck you and she wouldn't really make an effort to stop me putting stuff in her shaved little twat, and I'd say you're just a smack head Doll, doll hair, doll eyes.'

There were a few sexual encounters that year with other boys but I was apt to shock them with the sophistication of my tastes, especially fucking. My generation seems not to be as into it as much as Shamash's; it's one of those things either you get a taste for or you don't. I would find homosexuality quite inadequate as a sexuality if it didn't involve fucking, but that's just my opinion and fortunately it is one shared by enough of my brothers, as long as I remain comely I should be able to find boys with whom to do it.

147

Savant had me rowing up at the Hawkesbury most weekends and practising each day after school. Shamash would
come up and watch some Saturdays then take me back to
Paddington in the afternoon. I'd pig out on McDonalds all
the way back from Hornsby: milkshake, two quarter pound-
ers with cheese and large fries. Shamash would always sneer
at McDonalds and complain about the smell in the car but
still ended up eating half the fries.

'Why don't you get your own fucking fries, you always
eat mine and I'm starving after rowing.'

'You know I don't like McDonalds, just the fries now and
again, and my cruel child denies me a little sustenance after
a long drive to pick him up.'

'Yeah, well, I don't come into the Bayswater Brasserie do
I, and try and steal your "sauteed rack of dog's bollocks" or
whatever they have there, besides which I have to eat all that
shit at Savant all week. My God, the poshness ends with the
food Shamash, you should try it.'

'I went to boarding school too you know.'

'Not Shitsville though.'

'I bet our food was just as bad. It says in Savant's brochure they have trained nutritionists come in to help plan
the menus. We never had that. Why do you think I wanted
to get that scholarship to the Academy in London? How was
I to know that the food would be even worse there?'

'Dancing had nothing to do with it then, just food hey?
As for nutritionists at Savant – I don't think so. I think they
just pump the shit back up from the toilets and serve it to
us at room temperature, a totally self-sufficient environmen-
tally sound school. I should just get a hose and stick it from

my bum to my mouth, save 'em the prep.'

'Oh, Vas stop it. That's off.'

'Well, you should o' come down to Brighton and had tea with Mum and me, egg an' chips on a good night, greasy as old fuck, an' me Ma would o' shagged you an' all.'

'Vas don't talk about her like that mate, she was your Mum.'

'So I can say what I want. She never liked taking it up the arse though I recall.'

'Vaslav stop it.'

'Ere, I 'int Vas no fuckin' more I'm Johnny, HERE'S JOHNNY.'

Shamash hated it, hated me starting to be someone he had no control over, someone who only revealed himself when it was just the two of us. He hated it but I started to find it compelling. I began doing it all the time; it excited me. I was struck by the notion, at 15, that I was really a very interesting character, full of secrets, just waiting to be revealed, Mr Bloody Sophistication. I'd shock Shamash by talking normally while Thel was in the room then I'd notice her leave out of the corner of my eye and I'd answer the next question as Johnny: 'I don't want nuffink for me tea.'

It was like punishing Shamash for forcing me into a secret all those years ago, and it was a type of seduction, it was saying you're not my Dad, I'm something that's not looking for a Dad. It was just a game at first but it began to be a manipulative tool as well. Johnny wasn't fragile; he was the darker side and I was drawn to that side. At the time I yearned for darkness and intrigue and I still wanted to see Shamash's darkness.

He became concerned about my behaviour but once again didn't feel he could safely do anything so he became tense. He would ask me if I wanted to hurt him and I would always slip back into Vas and hug him and say of course I don't. I don't think 'hurt' was what I had in mind either, it was manipulation. I wanted to manipulate the safety out of my life.

I think I knew then that it was only a matter of time, a matter of wine, a project of mine.

JAMBALAYA

I got whisked out of school again. Savant made more of a fuss this time. I was already exhibiting signs that indicated education was not my top priority. I was 16 and starting to talk about leaving school, working in a shop. Shamash wasn't going to have a bar of that. He was rapt that he could afford to take me on the dance tours and hell, I wasn't likely to turn them down. He agreed I could start doing some work for Potts when we got back from the trip; that was the deal to keep me in school.

So it was Europe again and New York and London, and a couple of gigs in Rio at the last minute; five weeks in all. I was very nervous in England. I was also very bad. The cocaine was cheaper and more available. Shamash seldom had it in Australia but all the darlings of Bohemia over there never seemed in short supply. I was beginning to experiment with drugs; Vas did it in secret, but Johnny celebrated their discovery. That trip, that drug, was our real undoing.

The shows were brilliant fiery events. War was brewing in the Middle East, tanks could be seen on highways in the UK and Union Jacks hung patriotically in the windows of the council estates as we sped past in the car. There was something desperate and clichéd about Britain's response to that war. So the stage was set, literally and metaphorically, for the God of Sin to take another lover – a hungry bit of council estate white trash.

Poor Shamash, poor sweet Shamash who needed love so badly. He was sharing hotel rooms with me, we were alone, he no longer had any real control over me. He was being spoiled most nights by his various hosts; whisky and cocaine, expensive hotel suites with Laura Ashley drapery. In his brain that high-pitched coke buzz, in his heart palpitations of success and wellbeing, in his bed a fresh and filthy boy–child. My desires seemed to hang in the air, suspended by the heavy, artificial heat of the rooms.

I was so fucking horny I could have climbed the walls, fucked the floral Austrian blinds, cum all over the duvet. But I didn't have to, not in the end. The cocaine and whisky whispered other things to Shamash, things like, '*Now, now*, that's all there is, the moment, the flesh, you've done all you can. Look at him, so hungry for you, nearly out of his mind with lust. There's only one path of action, only one way to calm and soothe him. Shshsh to the white noise in your head, shshsh to all the confusion, only one thing to do, take your reward, your prize – what has been given you.'

'Try not to get worried . . .' That's what I sing to myself on the bad nights; that's what he used to sing when I was little. Lullabies become more savage as you get older. I understand now how, despite our love of gentleness, we want something else that's not so gentle, something that's part gentleness, part savagery. We loved each other, no question about that.

The love started quickly and hotly. Its residues unseemly on the prim English bedding, and we were not careful enough about returning to our separate beds. The housemaids doubtless gossiped.

I'm going to hot things up a bit here. Yeah I'll give you the sex. That's for sale and I was pretty hot. I was fantasy material, gaol bait. Maybe you would have gone to gaol, too. Maybe I was like a mermaid, a siren or just a whore you can't resist after drink and drugs. Vas doesn't get to write this, Johnny can take over. He's good at it, very good at it.

What I hate about the fuckin' Yanks and their porn is they have all this contrived bullshit dialogue, they make macho groans and yabber on in masculine monotones about what they're doing: *'Bug that arse man, fuck it, yeah, you fuck that tight arse.'* Never mind that the arsehole is as big as Texas and yawning like the Grand Canyon. Owen always says with an arse like that you'd have to throw a bone in there, send a dog in after it and fuck the dog before you'd get any service out of it.

You get service easily out of a 16-year-old and that's what I'm leading to. In the French porno films, the good ones, half the boys don't look any older than I was. In some of those, the boys look more like they're having surgery than sex. They get fucked and they yelp, yelp like dogs or moan in really uncontrolled ways. They're not contrived like the

Americans. I can't fathom half of what they say but it sounds better – they don't lie to each other. If they see an arsehole you could park the car in, they find another part of their partner to complement, his cock perhaps or his balls. If you get some piece of trash street hustler to be in a movie, you expect him to be a bit bruised, you don't get some sweet little pink puckered rosebud, you get the Chunnel. If you want convincing Catholic schoolboys with rosy cheeks and pouting perinea you go to a Catholic school. Shit, with the number of priests they charge these days, you'd think they were casting agencies anyway.

European porn is honest porn – unpretentious to boot. Their arseholes work for them. God knows how they do some of the things they do – drugs, I suppose. K is my bet – you could take on the football team after that wicked stuff. Sex is a different ballgame when you're on drugs, especially cocaine, which I had been getting into in London. I'd had some that fateful night, that first real time. Shamash must have known I was high when he came in, but what could he do?

Our sex was more French porn than American. (I prefer to think of myself as one of those Catholic schoolboys rather than the overworked street hustler but I have a place in my heart for both.) If my audience is going to fantasise then I can at least control the fantasy's direction. It was also more like *Endless Love*, the movie, which is a soppy comparison but I have to declare that so all homosexuals aren't eternally accused of being solely consumers of sex, of each other and of ephemeral attributes. But who the fuck isn't attracted to beauty? Owen reckons all arseholes smell the same so why do people bother looking at faces? My answer: Because all arseholes smell the same.

Sure, us men are animals at times, anarchists of desire. Perhaps we frighten the straights by making them think all men 'could' be like this. But Shamash and Vaslav/Johnny did love each other, and when that happens to male homosexuals, even for a moment, they don't walk away from it.

Shamash was more fey than the hobbledehoy. He was faced with losing another type of innocence. He was thinking about legal issues, social implications and his own spiritual failing as a father. Buzz buzz says the cocaine. Carefully, carefully shouts convention. The buzz won out. Johnny won out. Johnny all fresh and showered, all lubed up, reflected exquisitely in the wardrobe mirrors. The hotel, all cosy and flouncy while the December rain beat at the window. The wooden furniture, pot pourri and the metres of unnecessary fabric that covered every possible surface seemed loving and homely, not at all in tune with my desires. Shamash's coat (still the same one I saw that day at Victoria Station) was damp. He shuddered when he came in, and hung up the coat.

'You look rugged up, Vas.'

'I am,' I said, turning *Twin Peaks* down on the telly.

'Did you turn on my electric blanket on the other bed?'

'Forgot, Shamash.'

'You look altogether too carnal for me to give you a cuddle.'

'Pity. I wouldn't mind one.'

He looked puzzled for a second, then tired. Then the buzz from the coke must have kicked in again, and a rush of

155

warmth came over him. Still in his clothes, he pounced on me, tickling me like I was still a kid. I did a laugh that sounded like I still was. He cuddled me for a minute like I was his son. I let him cuddle me as if he were my father. For a minute my ribald calculations failed me; I wanted to be little again. For a thirty-second eternity I longed for my childhood and all its discarded wonders; its cosy security, its storybooks and fragility. But those yearnings passed as easily as the childhood that had treasured them. I had the coke buzz too, and when you're feeling that buzz any sort of physical proximity could turn into sex. Shamash moved to protest when my kiss to his cheek went searching for his mouth. I silenced him with the very kiss he tried to block. He sighed, I think in resignation, in desperation. I did my imitation of Scudder out of that film *Maurice*: 'Now we won't never be parted.' I did that in a Somerset accent, not council estate like Johnny.

There was romance in that line, a romance not lost on Shamash. In his heart of hearts he was always more enchanted by the notion of grand operatic passions, heaven and earth locked in battle with Valkyrian voices raised into a shrill aria that humbled the gods and opened gates to Vallhalla. He was more given to that notion than he was to my vulgar vaudeville of modern homosexuality: the painted faces and board beating, the rowdy show tunes and musty backstages of sex-on-premises venues. From that moment on he believed that line of mine; it signified an embarkation upon HMS *Impossible*, bound for uncharted lands, and the icy storm brewing in the distance was obscured by the ferocity of the heat we felt that night.

After that surrender, after we had both finally abandoned our 'feyness', he started to abandon his role as a parent. He became a lover, a savage one. We had to make every moment a unique one, an ecstatic one, a secret one.

Secrets. We had such a lot of them but this was the one I dreamed of. I longed to see him as a man not a parent. I desperately wanted to have that part revealed to me by him. I ached with joy when I finally whittled him down to it. His so-familiar face, his smell, his occasional awkward mannerisms – so strange in a dancer. I watched as lust overtook the melancholy in his eyes, as his tongue finally accepted my mouth's invitation and his unleashed strength and passion finally made him take me in his arms, like a baby, like Ashley had. At last he dominated me and our drooling cocks battled each other like angry dogs in a pornographic puppet show. His hands travelled down my back. They found the crack of my arse, and he felt the stickiness from the lube:

'You filthy bastard, you had this planned didn't you, Vas?'

'Not Vas, Johnny. I planned it an' all.'

'Don't start on the Johnny bit or that's the end of it, we'll stop here.'

'Sure Mar'in, like you could, ha bloody ha.'

And Johnny was right. He didn't stop.

Shamash fucked me three times that night. Something was being exorcised. I functioned like a well-oiled machine, at that age I was a well-oiled machine – everything worked so well, recovered so quickly.

There was I, a sweet, forbidden duvet delicacy, trained

up real nice by Ashley, used by a teacher and accomplice to a whore. I was a freak, no doubt about that, but there are always sluts, boy sluts, girl sluts. People love sex freaks, trash fucks, dirty young beauty; fresh filth-statutory rape-date rape, boy pussy surprise. The surprise being that the boy lets you have what he is expected to be still guarding, saving, valuing. Surprise is the new currency he's prepared to spend. Spend and spend. An arsehole that yields more than an ATM on a Saturday night. He is always two steps ahead of you in the seduction game. An irresistible nymph, an angel of lust sent down from heaven to provide pleasure to the deserving or an abomination to snare the morally somnambulant.

I could have made a career out of being fucked; perhaps I have. I could have been exploited beyond belief. Shamash could have sold me to some pornographer in Paris and I would have passed the last three years in a drugged stupor making porn movie after porn movie. They could have stuck bigger and bigger things up my arse until I ended up like one of those fist fuckees who almost prolapse when the fist comes out. You can get movies of that; I've seen them.

But that's not what happened. My sex, my uncontrollable libido was treasured by Shamash, kept secret and catered to by him only (for the most part). He let me reveal myself for what I was and he kept it safe. Yes he fucked me as hard as I wanted it. He went to the limits I demanded him to go to. Yes I probably made yelping noises and our lovemaking was full of saliva and lube and bodily smells. We shared extremes of intimacy. He would fuck me and say, 'Christ, Kiddo, what are we doing, this is no good, this is too good.' That trip was like a blur of sex, of reforming our

158

relationship. It was too good; we couldn't stop. I never even thought about stopping and Shamash knew that I was the weakness, that I was the risk. He had to fuck me and fuck me, push me like a wheelbarrow to my 18th birthday. I just wanted more sex, more love, more touching, and he always seemed prepared to bestow it on me, his twisted, monstrous child.

The change in our relationship kept me from going down to Taylor Square, where I could have been murdered, when we returned home. It gave me a new self-esteem. I was suddenly very grown up indeed. Short of slings and harnesses, you don't get much more grown up than we were in the bedroom. And yet we were both like children, too. When lovers reveal themselves to each other to the extent we did there's something archaic and remembered. Some halcyon spiritual recall.

'That's the garden, Darl, memories of the garden. Earth is but heaven seen through a glass darkly.' Brigitte's insights come to me at the strangest times, and of course the glass gets darker still.

I'm going to roll a joint now. I've said enough about that part. I think I could have given more close-up visceral shots, more pink flesh pull-backs as the hard penis enters and withdraws. I could have given you the meat stabbing which they give you in porn movies. That's the total withdrawal of the cock followed by its total re-submergence. Quick, short, sharp jabs, like a sword, in and out of a molten stone, thrusting forward and back accompanied by soft little wails from the one impaled. In and out goes the sword. The grail, the grail can be heard in the wail. But that's a porno technique for the benefit of the cameras and the audience. Once I had it inside I never wanted it to withdraw until it was finished. I would have thrust backwards to foil its escape.

I think about my story and wonder if I could sell it and demand they print it just as I write it. We like to think we're in control – all that shaping of your own destiny and reading the signs as they emerge. All that Brigitte stuff. But I wonder.

As the sexy dope fuzz starts to filter through me I decide it isn't really too late to go out. Not where I have in mind.

COURTNEY

'I never rooted him, he was kissing me, then he started fingering me, that's all.'

'You're a fuckin' slut Mandy, you'd go with any one, you would, bitch.'

On Saturday night these sorts of conversations can be heard clearly from my windows – so clearly that I can't help but get involved. There's a rawness and honesty to people's voices when they're on drugs. I can see them through the blinds; they think this is an unheard, private and ugly moment in their affair, but for me it's like watching a scary movie that I can't just turn off.

She's a pretty little girl with a sexy, heart-shaped face and a *Melrose* hairdo. I'd already be on her side if it were a movie – I always favour forgiveness when it comes to issues of infidelity. Her dress is one of those tiny satin shifts with shoe-string ties on the shoulder, her shoes strappy platform numbers, Joan Crawford style. He's a pumped up 'night wog', probably on steroids, which makes me wonder if he'll go into one of those 'roid rages. Already I can imagine the screams as he flings her about like a rag doll until she breaks.

'You were the one who told me to take that eckie, it just happened. Jesus Stav' can't you just forget about it? I'm still feeling sexy – let's go home, I'm not interested in anyone else. I love my big Greek sex god.'

She's trying to soften him up, her long red nails squeezing his biceps, reminding him of other delicious moments when he's been too caught up in her softness to notice their sharpness. She's rubbing the satin of her dress against his thigh. For a minute I think she'll succeed in taming him – she knows if she can arouse his desire the battle is half won. I feel for this girl, this poor straight girl who gets no scope in her life for any exploration. Love for them is a structured regime which even ecstasy has failed to loosen. Her reputation is at stake. He pushes her away. 'I don't want anyone touching my woman. You got that? You wanna be a whore, I just leave you here, teach you a lesson, slut.'

I hear him bleeping his car, a Mazda RX7 or something. He gets in, starts it up and screeches off down the road, away past all the other Saturday night casualties, past the bottles, vomit, syringes, condoms and dog shit that jostle each other for space on the Darlinghurst streets.

As the car roars off into the distance I am left with the sound of her whimpering on my front steps. Do I ask her in or leave her to the perils of the night? Wait to see a picture of her in a hopper or naked and trampled down one of the many lanes around here, so perfect for rape and murder. I imagine finding her little dress bloodied and smeared with dirt in my rubbish bin or being used as a gag by some brute while she sits shivering in her G-string lace panties, her knees locking together as she tries to protect that place that has already got her in so much trouble tonight. I am putting together an identikit picture of the monster who would turn this perfect-looking semi-durable commodity into fast food and litter. A nasty surprise for the council workers in the morning or an ashen-faced testament to the dangers of itty-bitty dresses, drugs and Oxford Street nightclubs. *Stop*, I scream to myself. I go and open the front door, startling her.

'I just heard all that. You wanna come in for a cup of tea? Can't sit there, you'll get trade.' I try to make my voice sound more poofy than usual so she won't think I'm a sex killer.

'Oh, God, I'm sorry. You forget people live in these places, I'm really embarrassed.'

'Don't be, I've been fingered by dozens of people when I'm on an eckie. He sounds like a right bastard.'

'Oh, he's really sweet sometimes, he's just possessive when he's pissed.'

'Well Hon, anyone who dumps his girlfriend in the middle of the night in these streets ain't worth it. Do you want me to call a cab?'

'No, it's alright, he'll be back – this happens all the time.'

'Fun game,' I say. 'Does anyone ever win?'

'Sometimes.'

So I'm sitting in the lounge at 2.30 in the morning wearing nothing but a sarong with this pretty bimbo who's too cute to really dislike but hardly what I'd call a soulmate.

I make tea, roll another joint when who should roll up but Essie and Macca (my abbreviations for Estelle and *Marie Claire*). Needless to say they don't like their nicknames but bugger them, if they want to turn up at all hours, uninvited, then I'll call them whatever I feel like.

'We saw your light on when we went past – we'd hate to miss any fun.'

They come in, *Marie Claire* dressed in a tight silver pant-suit with angel wings strapped to her back and swimming goggles dangling around her neck. Estelle shocks even me with what she calls her 'Barbie ensemble'. Her hair has been curled and dyed hot pink. On her head she is wearing a pair of baby's pink plastic pants with white lace trims and each leg hole has a pink ponytail pulled through it. She has a peek-a-boo midriff Barbie T-shirt (probably designed to fit a 6-year-old), shimmering with what she calls 'princess spangles', a shiny Barbie school-daze satchel and powder blue platform boots with pink pedal pushers that have 'Barbie's cunt' hand-stitched into the fly.

They've just been out to Kafae Phuc and performed a new 'piece' called 'Girlie Bitz', which apparently received a mixed reaction. 'It's full of suburban breeders on Saturday night,' says *Marie Claire*. I introduce them to Mandy, who has composed herself a bit, and I try to act like I know her, so she doesn't feel so bad about being dumped on the street like a prossie.

For some reason I've started to feel protective of Mandy, and when I notice she has one of those CC handbags I pretend to plump up a cushion and throw another one on the offending bag. I know how nasty those girls can get, especially when they've had a belly full of cocktails and God knows how much acid. The girls hone in on her, using their cosmetic consultant voices. I can tell she's more than a little intimidated.

'That's such a pretty little dress Mandy, issss that from Sssportsgirl or Portmansssss?'

'Portmans,' says Mandy, unsure whether Portmans is better or worse than Sportsgirl.

I glare at the girls in a 'just watch yourselves' sort of way. 'Mandy's just had a bit of a fight with her boyfriend.'

'He's my husband actually,' she says, as if that mere fact adds dimensions of safety and eons of certainty to her relationship. I think, My God, she couldn't be more than 20. 'This was supposed to be our six-month anniversary but I kind of fucked it up because of that eckie I had.'

'C'mon Mandy, he was being an arsehole,' I say.

'He just gets jealous, it's his insecurity. A lot of guys are really insecure in that way, I shouldn't of let him down like I did, I've just got this bad streak I haven't ironed out.'

'For Christ's sake!' cries *Marie Claire*. 'You're just a child, you shouldn't have to iron anything out, not even his fucking shirts. Girls should be allowed to do whatever they want and bastard men should only be given pleasure by women when it suits them.' She starts flapping her wings in an exaggerated way. 'Even then, stupid men should beg for it – like some dumb old dog for a juicy bone.'

'Juicsssssy juicsssy,' sings Estelle, stroking her curls and blowing a big pink bubble with her gum. It bursts and I can smell the artificial fruit flavour clear across the room.

165

Macca's even younger than Mandy. Mandy's looking at her like she's from planet Psycho-Les or something. Macca continues, 'All penetrative relationships are necessarily abusive, the penis knows only plunder.'

Estelle, who has been rocking to some secret music in her head and has hardly said a word so far begins to hiss from the couch. She has just discovered, and is now fingering disdainfully, the gold chain and leather threading of the handbag I'd tried to hide.

'Look *Marie Claire*, a Chanel bag. We love them don't we Puss?' Macca looks over at the bag, her face contorting.

'They look excellent next to a corpse.' Mandy is starting to get agitated and just then we hear the roar of the RX7 as it cruises the street looking for its missing accessory.

'That'll be Stavros,' she says, snatching the purse from Essie who then grabs her hand to look at the ring. '*Marie Claire*, look at the ring, it's beautiful isn't it?'

'Yeah, yeah, whatever,' Macca says, without even turning her head. She's busy peering out the window to see what the noisy black car is about to deliver. Mandy pulls her hand back, still naively unsure whether she's being flattered or insulted.

Mandy opens the door so Stavros can see her. He gets out of the car and lumbers across the street, a perplexed look on his dumb-fuck face. She's acting like nothing has happened earlier, like some sweet little wife with no desires of her own.

They wander back to the car, him muttering, 'Who were them weird chicks?' I can just hear her as she replies, 'I can't remember their names, one of them was called

Vanity Fair or something, I think they're lesbians.'

She's like me a bit – doesn't care so much about the cost, she wanted something and was not going to let her E go to waste. Who knows how long she'll put up with the abuse; perhaps that's their game, he goes off angry, returning to her when the rage subsides. Now she will be able to silence him with her tender little wet mouth, the one that doesn't have a voice of its own yet speaks loud and vulgar at times which don't suit her, times that endanger all of us, well me at least. A genetic weakness that ensures lots of people will want to have us but none will want to keep us. I wonder if people like us ever get control over those desires. Whatever the case, I'm stuck with the Darlinghurst Debutantes until their drugs wear off or until I fall asleep.

'Where'd you find her in that little Miss Fuck-me dress?' asks Macca.

'The storks delivered her to my door. It'll be all wet pussy and eckie talk for those two now they've had their little tiff. She loves him,' I say, mimicking her.

Essie starts singing '*I will hold, cherish and obey . . .*'

'What sort of stupid fuckin' bitch would agree "to obey" for Christ's sake? Not this little black duck that's for sure,' says *Marie Claire*, who orders Essie to get her some water while hunting through my CDs in search of Strawpeople.

I take another toke on the joint, wishing I'd made the most of the night. Essie has emptied her satchel on the floor. She has two Barbies in there, some tampons, cough medicine and several outfits for the dolls ranging from adventurous outdoor wear to glamorous Hollywood evening gowns. She

167

is deliberating over what the dolls' attire should be at 4 in the morning. Macca is trying to untangle the cord that makes her wings flap. 'Angel wings, cunts of things – 80 bucks, too.'

YABBADABBADOO

Sydney is like a prison to me. I can never believe I'm here. Why do I stay? Where else could I go? Selling tickets, programs and taking party bookings for Potts is not much job experience. If I were a waiter I'd go and work on a resort or something. But I am a prisoner. I'd last five minutes on an island; I'd be bored shitless. I need these stone wall streets now, the fuck clubs, the filth. I hate the city because I hate myself, can't live with it, can't live without it.

I'm coming down today, from speed, acid, alcohol and some unidentified sedative fed to me by a dubious acquaintance. I could tell when David came around that he was disappointed to see me hungover and still in bed at 11. Well I'm not his concern anymore and I can do without people fucking well judging me. I've only myself to blame; for everything it seems. Though I never betrayed Shamash again, at least not intentionally.

Last night I had sex with a number of people. I sat in the coffee bar at a sauna looking down through the glass floor at the pool below. I watched people swimming naked; it was like a David Hockney painting come to life. I was very out of it and when you're feeling like that you think everyone else is too. I manage, even shit-faced, to have safe sex (mostly), however I'm constantly amazed at how many people would happily indulge in the old-fashioned sort. You've got to have your wits about you or you'll find someone swallowing up your cock with their arsehole. Conversely you have to make sure none of those lubed-up dicks get up yours without a condom. It's a jungle in there.

At one point I found myself fist-fucking this guy. I've never done it before. He was one of those seriously heavy-duty dudes. I went into a cubicle where he was already displaying himself, amyl in hand. I was sort of getting into it with him but only half-heartedly, and I put two of my fingers into him; well next thing I know he's manoeuvred himself in this trick way and whammo, my whole fucking fist is up there. He hardly seemed to flinch and I sniggered to myself, thinking about Owen and the dog and bone business. The thing that amazed me, once my arm was in there, was how much space there seemed to be; it was like some vast chamber, one of those *Star Trek* black holes – a space–time continuum. I found the whole thing amazing in a really clinical, medical sort of way.

He was snorting amyl, allowing my fist to be the instrument that gave him some sort of isolated head trip, he was somewhere else – head surfing in a parallel universe. I thought how extreme this person's sexuality was, how his arse would be such a dud fuck, it would be like throwing a sausage down a lane. As I swivelled my fist around in there, I thought, He's spoiled himself for fucking, he has changed himself, stretched himself to such an extent that a soft, tight and gentle fuck would be quite out of the question. I twisted the huge loop of steel that pierced his nipple and only then did he groan. The drugs made me laugh; I was thinking, here I am, arm submerged nearly to the elbow in a position so powerful I could probably kill him, turn him inside out, and the only vocal response I get is when I touch his nipple.

I felt scared for that dude, scared by the vulnerability he allowed himself. It was the fist he wanted, not me, probably any fist would have done; fist and amyl were his tickets to nirvana. I withdrew my arm because the fascination passed. I realised that it was not a sexual thing for me, it was like doing an operation. It was the sort of thing Ren and Stimpy would do if they weren't on a kiddies' show. Drugs are bizarre; they turn moments of surrealist revelation, moments of utter debasement and depravity into some zany cartoon caper. Yabbadabbadoo.

I sat engrossed by the blue below, Dante's inferno. Down there a seething morass of lubricated muscle, skin and bone, a grown-up's party, flesh engulfing flesh engulfing flesh, the way *Alien* does, invading and redefining itself as it goes about its terrible business. I was contemplating how I love that sauna, how I love the safety of saunas, how I could stay there in the darkness forever.

I was tripping, thinking how I like this parallel universe that drugs turn on inside my head fuck – believing it was real, which it was at the time. Sometimes I can sit there feeling really sexy. Sometimes feeling like a little kid or an action super hero in a cartoon. One minute my dick feels like it belongs to someone else, next minute it's my actual soul. When that happens I suspect if anyone was to suck it too hard I'd get blasted straight down 'that' tunnel to heaven or hell or some fucking freak-out place. Other times it's different, like with acid when you're seriously shit-faced and some prospective piece of trade's blahing on to you about sex and whadda ya wanna do and d'you like t' fuck, and you're sitting there while they play with your cock and you don't mind but all you can think about is innovative cocktail glass designs or new concepts in semitrailer docking facilities.

That's how it was last night. I was just sitting there in the sauna, lost in ethereal steam not thinking anything, except, you know, buckets and spades, cars and trains, pixies and flowers. Some dude starts wanking me off. I wasn't that fussed but I let him because it felt like he had lube on his hand and that's a kind of nice and easy feeling, like having a little baby angel gently sucking on your soul. Well after a while it started to feel a bit sticky, like when you need more lube and I was thinking of moving on anyway. I pulled his hand away and as I did I looked at it through the mist and saw it was covered in blood. It wasn't lube it was fucking blood! I freaked right out. It was like waking up with a huge spider or snake on you. 'Are you crazy or what?' I shouted at him. He just grinned like an idiot. I headed for the shower. Then I started thinking maybe it was my blood not his.

So I'm trying not to freak right out in the shower, which is on display to everyone. I'm pulling back my foreskin to see if I'm cut in there, trying to see if I'm cut anywhere, on my balls or legs. Inside my head I'm saying 'Cool it, man', but part of me just wants to start crying because I've had such a fright. Other guys are looking at me which means I must be seriously agitated and I wonder if anyone saw the blood. I can't find any cuts and I start to wonder if there really was any blood. It's all gone, washed away down the drain. I look around, trying to see the guy from in the sauna. He's vanished. I shiver, cold and scared. If there was blood, why didn't he go to the shower to wash it off? There are no other showers he could use. I hate that sort of weird stuff, people looking at me like that, like I'm some sort of freak. Blood is not a thing guys want to see at a sauna.

Today I hate saunas, I hate the way they will always be there luring me into acts of sex, sometimes good sex, sometimes bad sex. I hate the fact that I have no control in that regard, that I am incapable of loving anyone new and even if I did, it would end up being in addition to those other things. Would Shamash have saved me from this? Who knows. We might frighten ourselves, us fags, but we are what we are and we do experience some extraordinary sensations in our endless pursuit of whatever it is we are looking for – momentary oblivion or eternal rest.

Hard to go back to school after the London scene. I thought I was hot shit that year; everything was boring, juvenile as far as I was concerned. Even Owen found me a bit up myself;

I was like a spoiled brat, a Texan girl. All the boys would watch *Capital City*, dreaming of their soon-to-be-realised business potential. Even I liked that show, but mostly Owen and I wanted to get stoned down on the oval and come back to our room to listen to music. We had a little bit of an overlap in our tastes so it was mutually agreed CDs we would play: Stone Roses, The Orb and sometimes he allowed Madonna, which we played only if we wanted to do really camp versions of 'Justify My Love'. What was never allowed by Owen was Pet Shop Boys or Kylie. I'd put them on and he'd go ballistic. I'd wrestle him so he couldn't get to the ghetto-blaster, I'd sing the words into his face, 'Better the devil you know, blah blah'. He'd pretend he was in physical pain at the sound of her. I'd prance about doing Pet Shop Boys' songs, 'Being Boring' was my favourite, and whatever else they might have said about me, no one could say I was being boring.

The other boys would bash on the walls. 'Shut up you fuckin' faggot, Usher.' That year the abuse seemed worse. I got bashed a few times. 'Your father's a fucking faggot and so are you Usher.' Faggette they called me. I didn't even deny it by then; in fact I played up to them, camped it up when they abused me: 'Usher, how the fuck did you even get born? You came out of some cunt's arsehole.' I let my work slip and got stoned whenever I could.

It was through this that some other bad business – the worst business – came to pass. One time I went on my own to have a joint at the local park. There is a public toilet block at the far side. I don't think it was a bona fide beat but I would always cast it a sidelong glance just to see if anyone was hanging around. On this occasion a guy was. The dope had made me really horny so I went over to check this bloke out. I was in my Savant tracksuit. That was my excuse if I got caught; I was jogging, 'Training, Sir, for inter-school.' Intercourse on this occasion was more like it. The guy in the toilets was pretty rough, with tats, which I loved, but not that good looking. I thought we'd just have a quickie, which we did, but he was dead keen to fuck me. I said no, just sucking. He wasn't easily discouraged however and twice tried to force himself into me. The second time he got in. I pushed him away and ran off back to the dorms. I really did jog that night.

The next night I wanted to go for a joint and this guy Stewart said he'd come with me. I suspected he might have wanted to kick some game, too. It's like, to do anything at that age you've got to get drunk or stoned so that if something happens there is a sense of diminished responsibility. He wasn't usually one of the dope smokers so I assumed a slight ulterior motive. I didn't particularly fancy this guy but I knew if I were stoned I'd be more keen.

I was more keen. He let me suck his 'famed' big dick and I actually talked him into doing the same to me. The trick was making sure you didn't make them cum; once they'd cum you wouldn't have had a chance. 'GAME OVER', says your internal Timezone. So I used to get them close then push their head down on me. They knew then if they wanted any more they'd have to give a bit of what they got.

We both ended up wanking off together. I could tell with Stewart that the sucking thing was a bit of a freak-out for him. He said quietly, afterwards, 'Is it true you have sex with your Dad?' I thought at the time sarcasm was still 'in' with the dickheads at school. 'Sure,' I sneered. 'All the time.' Perhaps the dope made sarcasm sound somehow earnest, perhaps Stewart was a bit dumb. I think, in retrospect, he was but of course his part in the incident was traumatic for him, too.

A couple of days later I experienced considerable discomfort pissing and a sore arse. I asked the matron if I could see the doctor. I didn't really suspect an STD but I thought if it was doctors had some oath or something that meant they had to keep stuff confidential. At that stage I had not experienced the more unpleasant consequences of sex, and I was woefully ignorant when I arrived at the clinic. I also thought the doctor had seemed okay when I'd visited in the past. A sprained ankle doesn't generate the same sort of inquiry as sore bums and infected urinary tracts.

It was gonorrhoea, and I had it in all three places. That filthy piece of Westie trash must have been ripe with it. Stewart also secretly took himself off to the same doctor, who found it in only two of the places. We should have got together and knocked up a story, nutted something out. The doctor at Savant's clinic was not as open-minded as some in Darlinghurst.

I said I got it from a girl, which of course was stupid considering I had it up the arse. Then I said it was another kid at school. 'You've been having anal sex, haven't you?' demanded the doctor. I didn't know whether he could actually tell or whether he was trying to intimidate me into an admission. He got his admission in the end but I ran out of lies to tell. I couldn't think fast enough and I said I didn't want to talk about it, that it was none of his business. I think that in itself was enough for him to start speculating about sexual abuse. Stewart told the whole story, however, and denied emphatically having fucked me. This left the question, Who did? Stewart probably said something like 'Kids at school reckon he has sex with his Dad', or 'He told me himself he has sex with his Dad', or some shit. Everything got very cloak-and-dagger after that. I didn't find out all the stuff until we were in court.

The doctor contacted my doctor, Shamash's friend Andrew, and discussed the issue with him. Andrew would probably never have been implicated in this whole thing had not one other unfortunate incident occurred. That same week, Shamash had acquired, coincidentally and without any contact with me, the very same complaint. He had gone to Andrew for treatment.

When I went home next weekend Shamash was very cool: 'We need to give it a rest Kiddo, for a little while.' We were both playing the same game. Andrew never told Shamash about me, and he didn't tell the doctor at Savant about Shamash, but all the necessary details were recorded on medical file cards. When required, Shamash's medical records were made available as well as mine. The evidence was all there. As far as the press was concerned, half the gay personalities in the city were allegedly involved in the porn ring. I'd been too vague and indecisive about where I'd contracted my dose of the clap.

Shamash pleaded guilty as years of circumstantial evidence mounted against him. My testimony, short though it was, only made things look more twisted, as though I'd been under some sort of Svengalian influence all those years. I emerged as a cross between Linda Lovelace and Pavlov's dog. 'It's best you say as little as possible,' said Shamash's lawyer.

I talked to Shamash, secretly, on the phone in the two months between the arrest and the arraignment. I stayed at Owen's place when I wasn't at school. Owen's mum was one of three 'temporary carers' who offered to look after me. Thel and David both offered, and I would have preferred either of them, but the court thought Owen's family the least implicated. Owen's mum was pretty spun out, especially since she'd got on alright with Shamash.

He stayed at Shadforth Street on bail until the journalists made it unbearable, until the disgusted neighbours and the empty theatre made it clear to him that Sydney was no longer his. AIDS organisations that he had funded wanted nothing to do with him so he booked into the Sebel under a different name and stayed there until they cottoned on and turfed him out. Down and down he went emotionally. He tried to phone me, but if I didn't answer the phone at Owen's he would just hang up. They suspected him of stalking me.

One Saturday, two weeks prior to the trial, Owen and I said we were going into town. I had managed to speak to Shamash on the Thursday and knew he was at the Hyde Park. I confided to Owen that I was going to see him and that he should wait in the park for me.

'You are so weird, man. If he's been fuckin' you, you should stay away, don't you reckon?'

'You don't understand, Owen. I love him, I'm all he's got.'

178

'Yeah but if he loved you he wouldn't fuck you, not his own kid. You will have some serious shit in your head after all this Vas, you'll be nutso.'

'Is that what you think, cunt?'

'Hey man, I don't think anything. I always liked your ol' man. I just can't get over all this. How long's he been fucking you? It's gross. Like he's okay looking and that but he's your Dad for Christ's sake. I'd freak if my old man tried it on with me. Barf.'

'I don't want him to go to gaol Owen, but there's nothing I can do. I just want to see him, one last time.'

I guess it was like cinema that meeting, like some tragic war-time romance where the hero was doomed. I suppose I fancied myself as one of those women who was prepared to throw aside conventional morality and fuck him before he died. I thought we could have made love, hugged, cried, held each other desperately. Of course it didn't turn out that way. No last cigarette, no train departing, no parting glances.

I thought how ironic that it was the Hyde Park Plaza again. I went under-cover in one of Owen's baseball caps, the right way around, unlike the way Owen wore them. I couldn't get in the lift fast enough. I got to Shamash's room and he opened the door. He was hideously drunk, his face red and tear-stained. He broke down as soon as he saw me.

'Oh God Vas, what have I done? I just want to die, I'm just going to keep drinking until I do.'

The room was a mess, like some sort of lair, and the do-not-disturb sign had probably been on the door since he arrived.

'I have to plead guilty Vas, there's no way around it. I wish they had the death sentence. I wish I could be hanged.'

'Stop it, stop it,' I wailed through my own sobs. 'I'll testify that I was out of control, that I was a drug addict. I'll say anything that might help.'

He sobered up for a second, though he was swaying. He looked at me with this perplexed expression on his face, this expression of disbelief, of near loathing.

'Are you mad, Vaslav? Johnny? Whoever the fuck you are. It wouldn't make a shit of difference what you said, it wouldn't matter if you said you'd raped me. My life is over, Vas. I'm fucked fucked fucked. I am a piece of living shit, a sarcoma on the face of homosexuality and a blight to fatherhood, to man-fucking-kind. Just go, Vas, and try to have a life for my sake. I'm over talking now, I'm drinking to try and get over thinking.'

I tried to hold him but he sort of shook me away.

'No Vas, no cuddles, no more, no more love, no more sex, no more no more.'

And he collapsed and wept as if he might, at any moment, die. He let me hold him then and we both cried and cried until there was a bash at the door.

'We believe the boy is in danger being here Mr Usher. You know a restraining order has been issued against you and you are currently forbidden from having any contact with your son. If anything like this happens again we'll have to take the boy into protective custody and you will no longer be eligible for bail. Do you understand?'

Shamash was still weeping, but sort of laughed. 'Yes

officer, I forgot how dangerous I was, how frightening to young boys, how vile.'

One of the hotel staff had come to investigate and called the police. Of course Shamash was kicked out of there as well after that incident. He ended up somewhere in the Blue Mountains, Leura I think, in a motel. Somewhere he wasn't recognised, somewhere to stay until the trial.

The police took Owen and me back to his place but not before some journo, who had somehow found out about the incident, snapped my picture as I left the hotel with the cops. Everyone knows that photo – my face all blotchy and agro, my fingers doing the 'get fucked' gesture. That picture won some fucking award, ended up on a CD cover for a band I hate, on the cover of a book about child abuse. You can plaster it wherever you like as long as you pay the newspaper for the rights. It made some cunt famous and became my nemesis. These days David tries to make light of it, calls it my 'Jackie O', but I can't make light of that picture even now because that day was, perhaps, the worst day of my life.

Thelly had to reveal things in court that broke her heart. She wasn't up to the fierce questioning she underwent:

'So Mrs Dawson, you never thought it strange that Vaslav continued to sleep with his father, continued to sleep with him even as a teenager?'

'They were very fond of each other. There was quite a bit of tragedy in their pasts.'

'But even so Mrs Dawson, a 15-year-old boy being taken out of school to go abroad each year. Would you have done that with your children at that age?'

'If I'd had the money I dare say I would have.'

I don't think Thel understood. She certainly hadn't known Shamash and I were lovers, but I could see from her face that once she realised he had been 'doing the nasty' with me, she tried to sound as if even that was forgivable. If anyone was to be really disgusted she was the one I could most easily have forgiven, but she wasn't. She knew there was something wrong with the case. She also knew something else.

It got worse and worse for Thel. She said I'd always seemed like I was going to be gay, that I was 'theatrical' like my father. No matter what she said it seemed worse for Shamash. In court he just sat, ashen-faced. He looked so miserable; I watched him thinking he would die from his broken heart. He wouldn't look at me in the courtroom.

Shamash confessed that he had sodomised his own son – he would have pleaded guilty to mass murder by that stage. On the final day he said, 'I'd like to explain something ... no ... there is no point ... it's a monstrous crime.' As he said this he finally looked at me.

BUSHED

Shamash rang me today. He sounded out of it.

'Hey Vas, remember that night we went to The Fridge in Brixton? Remember how they weren't going to let you in, they didn't think you were 18?'

'Well I wasn't. You said I was a dancer from the company and all "your" dancers were over 18.'

'And that guy at the door said if we were really dancers we should give them a show, and they called other bouncers over to watch, and I said we'd do something from *Hatstand & Codpiece* direct from Adelaide.'

'Direct from Ada-where?' the bouncer had said. I laughed. 'And I got to play the hatstand 'cos I couldn't dance.'

'You could dance, you just never tried. Remember that Celtic proverb I had? *Never give a sword to a man who cannot dance.*'

The line went quiet, and I finally spoke.

'Shamash, do you think things will be alright one day?'
He didn't answer for a long time.

'I don't know, Hon.'

'I still love you for what it's worth. You know David and I will be here for you – Shamash, I'm writing about it all.'

'You're writing a book?'

'I'm sort of just doing it for myself at the moment. Brigitte reckons it would be worth a lot of money to publish.'

'I suppose it would. You should write a book.'

'I could just sell the story to *Who*.'

'Jesus, don't do that. We get that in here.'

'Alright, I'll write a book about it. Maybe when you come out we can launch it?'

'It's not going to take that long to write is it?'

'You'll be out soon.'

'Don't hold your breath. Please not *Who*, whatever you do. Write a book. Or is it the money? You want more money? I'll talk to the solicitor.'

'I don't want more money, I'll write a book instead.'

'Yeah Vas, a book's better. You just stick at it hey and write something thorough. Maybe you can show me first. I don't like what those magazines do. Hey I gotta go, someone's hassling me to use the phone. Maybe you'll come and see me soon?'

'You want me to?'

'Yeah, soon.'

Shamash is 38 now, and if he's lucky he might get out after his 40th birthday, but I've been told not to count on it. He might have to wait until he's 45. He already looks that old anyway, in his face at least. His body he keeps up, he can work out; I think that's the only interest he has anymore. Even that he does out of habit, out of some sort of mechanical need to affirm to himself that he is in fact still alive. I suspect he's on drugs, too. Apparently they get smack in there. I suppose if I were Shamash, if I had as much future as he sees himself as having, I'd be on it too. Smack is perfect, perfect for when there's nothing else. I amaze myself that I haven't dabbled more than once or twice. I've always wondered if I were one of those babies born addicted to the stuff, but I suppose Mum probably didn't get on to it until after she had me.

I rang Owen. Said I wanted to go out drinking. I had the money. There are times when a boy needs to go on a bender, and this was one of them. Owen had been bonking this feral dude called Riz so he dragged him along as well. Riz is the kind of guy who really fucks me off. He's the type of self-professed radical who walks into cafes or bars and picks up people's mobile phones and pretends to talk on them. It was really embarrassing and not the sort of crap I felt like going through. He'd pick them up and say, 'Hello, I'm a big fat capitalist wanker and you're speaking to me on my penis extension.'

Needless to say, the dudes who sit with their phones on the table don't like that sort of thing. They also don't have any respect for dickheads like Riz. We should have gone to Newtown where people still use phone boxes. We mightn't have got kicked out of two cafes that way. I was the one buying their drinks. Owen kept pretending it was cool and funny, the way Riz was going on, but Owen comes from a wealthy family, too. While Riz was taking a piss I said to him, 'The only reason you can afford to slum it is because your folks are loaded. That guy's a dickhead.'

'Well at least he doesn't wax himself and sip cocktails like a girl.'

'He couldn't afford cocktails unless I bought 'em for him – he's fucked, he's a tosspot.'

'Yeah right Mr Together Fuckin' Dude. Excuse me while I just go home and root my old man.'

I walloped him across the face, sort of a slap more than a punch. I knew I was going to punch him up or burst into tears so I ran off, leaving them with a bill to pay, which I knew they couldn't afford. I felt really crappy and thought all I can do is write a fucking book. That's all I've got, that and a bunch of stupid airhead friends who think my child-hood is just some elaborate plot device.

About half an hour later Owen turned up with flowers he had stolen from the supermarket around the corner. He sort of hugged me and said sorry. The two of us sat around drink-ing what was left of some vodka I had in the freezer and smoking dope. We played the mind game we used to do at school called Cardiac Arrest. We would try to talk each other into believing our hearts were slowing down. It used to freak us out when we were stoned. I told him about Mandy and the 'night wog', and Estelle and Macca's reaction.

'That Estelle, she's a fruitcake man, she's like one of those babies born without a brain.'

I sniggered, 'I s'pose she got *Marie Claire* instead.'

'I'd rather my own brain thanks. I wouldn't count on ol' Macca to save the world.'

'Well we're hardly going to save it ourselves, are we,' I muttered into the stinky old bong.

'We're not here to do that, leave that to the mobile phone dudes and dudesses.'

'Maybe them saving the world is like Shamash saving me.'

'How'd he ever save you? he got you in deep shit.'

I didn't answer.

We listened to Stone Roses and it was just like old times. As Owen lay there he said, 'You know, when we were at school and I'd come over to your place I used to think about your Dad, like for sex, I reckon I would'a done it with him.'

'Owen, I guess there are a few things you should know. Number one, he's not really my Dad.'

Owen looked at me in disbelief. 'Whadaya mean?'

And off I went again.

After the court case I lived at Thelly's until school went back. David was deemed an inappropriate guardian and Rosie was relieved at Thel's offer. I was, too. It meant I could go and live in Homebush where I wasn't such a 'celebrity'. I wasn't allowed to see Shamash until I was 18 but I was virtually compelled to see the shrink; even Thel thought it was a good idea. He was like a vulture that man, slick, clever and utterly depraved. When he gave me the tranquillisers, when Johnny emerged to protect Vas from having to expose himself

187

emotionally to the doc, well it was on for young and old. When I told him of my sexual exploits, of my infamous libido, when I told him these things the way Johnny would see them, as lascivious tales to drool over, as phone sex, as 'come on, don't you want to play with those young sticky bits that have been up for grabs for years', when I did that, his Freud and Jung seemed to fly out the window.

Gradually the style of therapy changed too; it became more sedated and more tactile. I didn't even care at the time. I laughed at how perverse this whole arena of behaviour was. It seemed impossible to me that something like that could happen. I guess then I thought, 'Just do what they want, try to enjoy it, be a blameless whore. I couldn't tell Thel about it. I didn't want her to be any more upset than she had been. Besides the easiest thing for me to do was just have sex with people when they required it. I found it easier to have the sex than not to. I still find it easier to have sex than not to, but it is on my terms these days.

When the holidays ended I was supposed to go back to school, this time the local school. I told Thel I didn't want to and she said she couldn't make me. I told her I was going to find a job somewhere, eventually. David had power of attorney for Shamash, which really pissed Rosie off. He was ordered to provide for me from the rent on Shadforth Street. There were provisions made for university, but that never came about; I've already pissed that money up against the wall. I've always had any money I needed. I try not to take very much, just what's required for this dive. I do work when there's a show on. I guess I liked being over in Homebush for a while. Thel went and worked at some gift shop in

Burwood after we left Paddington. She never minded me just hanging around watching vids and getting stoned. She'd nudge me a bit: 'Vas, why don't you get a job a couple of days a week? I'll talk to Dorothea at the shop if you like. She needs someone to unpack stock.'

'I'm not working in some old lady's gift shop.'

'Well a cafe. Go up to Newtown, there's lots of cafes opening up there. Dianne's always on about them.'

After a while I got bored with dope and 'therapy'. I caught the train into Newtown and went into this groovy-looking cafe called Vesuvius on the off-chance. They gave me a job washing dishes straight off. I got into a bit of a scene down there; it was alright. People in Newtown are more laid back. On this side of town people give you about two seconds of smiles and eye contact; they can work out if you're worth their time in less than that. In Newtown they've got a bit more time for you.

Thel had been great but I started to realise I could do whatever I wanted, even move out if I felt like it. She had her film nights and leagues club dos and I wanted more inner-city action. The law had finished with me, processed me, and Shamash was really the only person who had ever given a stuff about me being educated. I'd never put much stock in it myself.

I moved into a share house with all these hippies and neo-punks. I wasn't into all their radical politics but when you're in a house like that you just agree with stuff and have another bong. I think it was my dope they were usually more interested in than their anarchism and revolution, anyway. They were all older than I was.

I ended up waiting at Vesuvius; it was going okay. I'd been there about six months when they accused me of stealing 10 dollars from the tips. It was fucking outrageous. I never stole that money; if I'd wanted money I could have got it easily, I even offered to give them 10 dollars if they wouldn't believe me but they sacked me. Gareth the arsehole manager then went and employed his best friend. I think that was when I really had a breakdown. It was so awful. I just felt like a little kid again, a kid with no Mum or Dad or anything. I walked all the way along King Street crying and shaking. I couldn't stop and people all stared at me. I felt like throwing myself under a bus or something. Destiny, this Goth chick from our share house was coming the other way. She put her arm around me and took me home but it was no good. I felt like I would be depressed forever, like I needed to be put in some sort of home, an asylum or something.

That was when I started really getting into the tranquillisers. I rang David and asked if I could come and stay. He agreed and I packed my bags and came 'home', wherever that was.

The depression continued for months. That was when I tried to top myself. That's when David saved me. I'd have killed myself by now if it weren't for him. It makes you wonder about a psychiatrist who prescribes 'minor tranquilisers' to an 18-year-old who has just been legally orphaned by the authorities, who was clearly quite traumatised by the whole scenario. David was supposed to be away in Melbourne for two days but he came back early and found me.

It's strange but when I took all those pills it didn't seem cataclysmic; I just felt sad and tired. I couldn't see anywhere to go and because he saved me I feel guilty now about what I put him through as well. I didn't want to do that and Shamash, what would my suicide have done to him? I can't think about that; I feel so ashamed now. It becomes apparent that life's not through with me yet, that I, good, bad, responsible or not, am here to stay, for a while at least.

And that brings me to here, where I've been ever since. Near agoraphobic in a three-room flat in Darlinghurst, which is the exact same situation my mother had at the same age. I've come full circle. Even platform shoes are back in. I hear that haunting clomp outside my window, and I think of all the fresh whores out there. All the whores with weighted feet clomping their way to ruin. I think how lucky I am that I'm not dependent on the slickness, the tightness, the currency of my own arsehole to keep me in food and shelter. I don't have to suck old codgers' cocks or give myself injections twice a day. I have been provided for. I am a kept boy. I am a lucky boy.

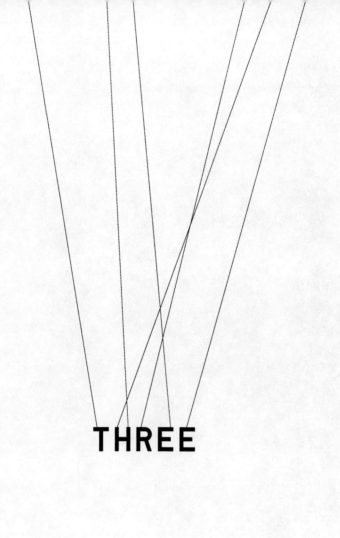

THREE

N E W S

*Sydney's arts community today mourns the passing
of one of its great performers and entrepreneurs, Martin
Calvin Usher. The former Director of Potts En Pointe Dance
Company and a highly publicised spokesperson for the
Sydney gay community died yesterday in the Goldstone
Detention Centre.*

*Prison spokesman Mr Arthur Pembroke said a full inves-
tigation of the death would be undertaken, though at this
stage there appears to be no suspicious circumstances. In a
statement issued to the police last night he concluded by
saying, 'Mr Usher had been suffering severe bouts of depression for some months prior to his death and had already
withdrawn himself from most prison activities. He was a
gentle and popular prisoner with staff here, we are all very
shocked and saddened by his sudden death.' Prison officials
have decided no further statements will be issued until the*

coroner's inquest has been completed and, if necessary, a hearing surrounding the incident has concluded.

The Usher family have chosen to hold a private funeral ceremony at an undisclosed church and no statements from family members have been made at this stage. Martin Usher will be remembered for his generosity and artistic vision. His annual KICK-BACK benefits raised in excess of $700,000 for AIDS charities throughout the 1980s. It is hoped his memory will live on through many more performances at Sydney's much loved Wylde Street Theatre.

Usher's business partner and artistic collaborator, David Bergdorf, said from the steps of his Elizabeth Bay home, 'We were the dearest of friends for nearly twenty years. It was the press who conspired to destroy him three years ago, so I don't care to dignify any of you with tales and sentiment now.' Fighting back tears he added, 'I believe in the fullness of time the people of Sydney will come to understand Martin Usher the man and truly mourn his tragic and premature demise. He was a fine man in spite of all the events that culminated to have him seen as otherwise. That is all I have to say.'

PORT JACKSON DAILY   14/11/94

I don't move from the floor. An exotic-looking arts journo on the ABC is standing outside the Wylde Street Theatre looking towards Woolloomooloo. The Bridge and the Opera House can be seen in the distance. She's talking about Sydney's artistic past, its scandals and misunderstandings.

She had just finished going on about some witch called Rosaleen Norton whose paintings were banned because they thought she was a devil worshipper when in fact she was a pagan and her depictions were of Pan not Beelzebub. She talked about Brett Whiteley's heroin addiction and showed footage of Wendy Whiteley being arrested at customs for drugs or something. Then it was some Danish architect who designed the Opera House and got shitty with the builders because they cut back on the budget for the project and he pissed off back to Denmark. The program's called *Artributes* and the story of Shamash was to be tonight's 'feature':

> *It has been suggested that under current funding legislation, a company like Potts En Pointe would have an uphill battle establishing themselves today. When Martin Usher and David Bergdorf first joined forces, they had plenty of obstacles in their path but as this interview from TDT in June 1981 shows, they were not going to be put off easily.*

They were in flouncy dinner shirts and Shamash looked as if he had eyeliner on; they looked more like Spandau Ballet than entrepreneurs negotiating funding and council permits. Their hair was gelled, their suits expensive and elaborately cut. It was just a few months before he had gone to England to get me. Shamash was first to speak.

> *We have already seen the Woolloomooloo council getting 'matey' with developers. Permits have been consistently granted for enterprises with far less community support than ours. Council has barely stopped short of totally destroying the entire suburb. It has even been suggested people have been done away with so development proposals can proceed unhampered. We're merely trying to get a small liquor licence*

to serve drinks at interval and prior to shows. (A cute, mischievous-looking David butts in. He had a lot more hair then.)

It is quite likely after the Juanita Nielson affair our lives are in danger for coming on this show. (They laugh momentarily, then it was back to the journo.)

Well it wasn't all laughs for Usher and Bergdorf. As the eighties progressed the Sydney gay community felt the full impact of the worsening AIDS crisis. Usher also lost both his parents in the notorious Millionaire's Club flight bound for Antarctica. It was only through the pair's tenacity and innovation that Sydney's leading contemporary dance company weathered the storms of what theatre critic Felicity Duplaix describes as 'the dynamic and unforgiving arena of performance art'.

Usher's life was fraught with tragedy and as one of the country's biggest media scandals was brewing, silently, behind the closed doors of his magnificent Paddington home, the shows just seemed to get bigger and better. (The journo started talking to Felicity Duplaix, leading art critic and editor of *Stage d'Or* magazine.)

As a dancer Martin was one of our best. I saw a great many of his shows here in Sydney and abroad, and the Wylde Street Theatre is the best space in Sydney for contemporary dance of the Potts calibre. I think much of Usher's torment was evident in his dance, and excellence perhaps needs a broader moral meadow, as it were, to manifest itself in. There was a savagery and anarchy in Martin's movement that I haven't seen since on the Australian stage. His other great skills of course were choreography and management. Very few

people had his capacity for fundraising. He was an extraor-
dinary figure, a very kind and generous man. I, like most of
Sydney's arts community, am deeply saddened by his death.

'He never liked you much Flis,' I mumbled to myself. 'Felicity
Duplicity he used to call you. He'd read your editorial *Screen
d'Or* to David in that husky plummy voice.' I started to cry
again.

I tuned out, digesting words until they became abstract
sounds without meaning, floating around in my head –
'brewing behind closed doors'. The telly was skipping from
snippets of different shows to Mardi Gras to David and
Shamash getting a Premier's Award in 1989. Then the camera
followed them back to our table in the Darling Harbour Convention Centre where I was sitting next to Ashley, both of
us kissing both of them.

The camera focused on me kissing Shamash. Then they
froze it and zoomed in. The footage wasn't brilliant quality
to start with so the more they tried to zoom in, the more
pixilated and disturbing the image became. It was as if they
were giving the audience the chance to search my face for
any signs of the corruption that was already 'brewing behind
closed doors'. Even I was looking for signs by the time they
suddenly shattered the still as if it were a family photo that
had been carelessly knocked from its pride of place on the
sideboard. I got a fright when they did it. At the same time
someone kicked my front door, yelling some incomprehen-
sible abuse. I froze where I was, watching the TV version of
my life flash before my eyes. I couldn't turn it off, even
though I knew it would upset me. Now the journalist was

standing outside Goldstone, her red lipstick and trendy clothes completely out of place in that shit hole.

Usher pleaded guilty to four of the charges brought against him and for the last three years this austere penitentiary in Sydney's outer western suburbs has been his sole place of residence. A sombre reminder of one of society's most feared and least tolerated offences. Many questions remain unanswered about the extent to which Vaslav Usher was abused by his father, and allegations of child pornography rings headed by Martin Usher have proven to be largely unfounded.

Questions surrounding the age of consent for homosexuals recur from time to time in the press but one thing is for sure, incest remains taboo and childhood sexual abuse the last frontier of moral transgression. (Suddenly the journalist was in Oxford Street, surrounded by trendies just like herself.) *Here, in Oxford Street, site of the world-famous Sydney Gay and Lesbian Mardi Gras, attitudes seem to be a little more relaxed. In fact several family law specialists say that in cases like that of Martin and Vaslav Usher, there are a number of possible solutions.* (She turned to a smartly dressed lawyer who got to say his bit.)

In a less public case there may have been the possibility of a reconciliation between Usher and his son. The real damage in a scenario like that one was the public nature of the case. Many families have hidden dynamics that aren't easily explained and often fall foul of the law. Where we can we attempt to work with those families. There is often an opportunity to repair or at least reconcile some aspects of the damage that has been done.

The reality is, with many crimes of this nature, the only chance to minimise the damage caused, is through discreet, unpublicised counselling and privately mediated discussions between the parties involved. Neither Usher nor his son were given the remotest opportunity to achieve this; in fact, after Martin Usher's conviction, Vaslav was not even allowed to see his father until he was 18. Needless to say I think it will be a long while before the press are likely to have any concern for the lives they meddle in when it comes to issues as inflammatory as paedophilia and incest. I think the climate of moral panic is far too hot at the moment to let anyone off the hook, and if the press really did have humanitarian concerns for the victims of crime they wouldn't have subjected Vaslav to what they did. (The lawyer looked back to her. She was smiling and nodding in a way that tells us she would never be one of those journalists. We cut to Taylor Square.)*

Usher's friends and family have declined to appear, but those who know Vaslav Usher say he is deeply grieved by the loss of his father.

Then 'they' came on and I felt a wave of betrayal and loathing. Those two witches, sitting outside Cafe 191 wearing something halfway between mourning and bondage. Estelle had been pushed into the background as usual by Marie Claire (fuck her italics, the bitch can go without). She looked at the camera.

We haven't known Vas for that long, maybe six months. He's a very sensitive and kind guy but you can always see that

*hurt – the hurt from what happened to him. We don't know
his father but he was still very fond of him. I think they had
a bond that challenged even the expanding definition of
'queer', it certainly went beyond the bourgeois sentiments of
most current affairs shows, if you know what I mean.* (The
journo was nodding like she did know what Marie Claire
meant.) *It's very hard to establish yourself as a performer
when you're gay or lesbian. Estelle and I have both learnt
that as performance artists there are a lot of people who can't
see past the moral paradigm established by American sit-
coms and as Thespian lesbians of the millennium we think
that sucks.*

Estelle started to make a sucking sound in the grim residue
of her drink and the camera honed in on the straw vacu-
uming up the murky sludge from some unidentifiable fruit
juice. It seemed mine and Martin's life had just been gurgled
up a straw into Estelle's mouth. The camera cut back from
the journo to the presenter.

*Goodbye Martin Usher and hello to the Thespian lesbians of
the millennium. To just what extent does art redefine morality? Is it ethically legitimate to reflect on varying forms of
moral reality through performative expression? Next week we
delve into the sticky questions that surround that very issue
in Artributes.*

I just lay there exhausted. I bet those girls conned the ABC
into getting onto that show. I wished they'd been cut;
those idiotic bitches will do anything for attention. Brigitte

called and said come over, come and stay for a few days.

I still can't let myself accept the death and how horrible it was. Shamash's death has been accepted as a suicide by the prison but nasty questions surround this 'suicide'. The biggest and most horrific being the fact that something had been inserted into him, anally. If it hadn't been for a careless statement by the coroner when David and I went to see the body, this fact would have been suppressed, too.

Shamash wouldn't do something like that; he wouldn't stick a bottle of fucking hair conditioner up himself and then hang himself. Who for Christ's sake would? David had to give me sedatives when he got me home; I was sick with grief and anger.

I don't mind crying in front of Brigitte. She knows exactly the sort of guilt and fear I'm suffering:

'Yes Darl, horror is real but it's not real for Martin anymore. All the horror is over and done with for him now, and Sweetie you can't take all of this onto yourself. You can't be the one to carry all his guilt as well as your own for the rest of your life. It seems you've had more than your share in this life Darling Heart but that's what life is for. It's a forum for horror, it's a play where we get to explore every type of dynamic and deceit; There is no hell Vas, this is it. You are in hell now and gradually you will rise up out of it. You've got to do that for your Mum who never had the chance, for Martin who loved you and for me and David and Thel.

You see, Darl, we're all just a house of cards really, and

if we fall down we take everyone else with us. You forgive Martin, he forgives you; no one else matters. The law might judge us but I doubt God does, he leaves us to our own devices down here. It's us that have to forgive each other and in that sense we get to play the role of God too. Think of being old and having such a past that you'll be notable as well as notorious – that wicked Vaslav Usher, heir to Sydney's most decadent Bohemian fortune. You'll be more famous than Rosaleen Norton.

You see we need darker heroes, too, Vas. People probably admire them the most secretly. You should aestheticise your life just like your Shamash did with his. The apple's only half-eaten – take another bite, Darl.

PETHIDINE

'Grief and death were born of sin, and devour sin,' Brigitte tells me. It's a quote from St John Chrysostom. She always goes and gets someone else to back her up, even if it's someone who's been dead for five hundred years.

I wonder if anyone has any idea what it would be like being in my situation. I suppose some do. Betrayal is infinite and sin is as random in its selection of perpetrators as HIV is in its selection of infectees. I am a total mess. I feel like the focal point in some vast cosmic enactment of an ancient moral tale that has come to rest. It's as though I'm living out some perpetual myth or scriptural illustration, but I know fuck-all about Scripture and I don't have Brigitte's interpretive skills. Fuck your way out of this one Johnny boy.

I wonder if I should listen to Brigitte. I don't know if she has real messages from the other side – from through that glass that is so dark now it's black. I used to try to visualise it while I was in the bath or stoned. I could see glimmers of movement through the steamed-up mirror or the translucent shower screen. Brigitte taught me that by focusing on things, using the other side of my brain, I could see glimpses of the 'other side'. It seemed to be true, too.

For a while I saw flickers, shadows – possibilities. I couldn't identify them or make them out clearly the way Brigitte does, but it did seem like there was something to the idea. Now I feel locked into myself, forced into some human dimension in which I must endure mental and physical agony for some period of time I know will be longer than I can bear. That's why I've been rocking myself for so long, hugging the pillow. And then it comes again like an attack. The thought of Shamash having to go through whatever it was someone made him go through. And I can't stand to think of a group of them pushing that bottle into him and then making him hang himself. I can't stand thinking about how scared he would have been, how much pain he endured and the dignity he lost. It's like a scenario I have to go through time and time again, each time weeping and rocking; it's like sickness or a fit, imagining his face. Him crying, screaming. Going through his greatest horror some-where else, without me. Like I would have been any help anyway – dream on, Vaslav.

Maybe he was over me. Maybe I'd exhausted him, taken his will away. He may have wondered how he would ever get rid of me, like I was a really bad mistake he made. I was a bad mistake for him. He never got enough good out of me in thirteen years. That's how many years it was when he died. I wonder if I'm some sort of beast. I don't want to be.

Brigitte tries to 'talk me back', tell me I'm loved. But I don't know whether it's true. I don't know who could love me. No one loves you if you don't love yourself, any fool knows that. If I survive all this I wonder what use I'll be to anyone. That's what I keep thinking: What use am I? What good am I? Who will really want me and how?

I feel like I've been born into a nightmare. I see myself as a 7-year-old on Victoria Station, hoping my Mum will wake up. Knowing she won't. Knowing something bad, feeling the weight of my life get heavier and heavier. I never meant to hurt anyone, really I didn't. Ashley hurt me. He shouldn't have messed with me. He should have left me alone even if he saw what I was like. It's like all these people have got inside me and messed around with bits of me and now I don't work properly anymore. Like I'm a person who's not quite right in the head. Then, when I think that, I get really scared because I think I don't have a chance like other people.

And that Johnny is not worth the council estate he slouches about in. He says stuff like 'It's just you and me mate against all 'vem uver cunts', but he's not real and he hasn't done me any good so far. I have to try to believe Brigitte 'cos even if she's wrong she's older. She knows more than me and maybe she is the extra help I need. I guess I love her, too. Right now I need a Valium even though I shouldn't have them with Prozac. Like I give a damn. I am deeply fucked.

We will have the funeral tomorrow at some Anglican church in Mosman. Rosie reckons it's the family church but I can't remember ever going there. I won't argue with her; I can't face her at all. David has organised it with her and I am very scared about going. Shit scared. I want to disappear but I'm not well enough mentally or physically to go anywhere yet. I wish I could just die. Everything is all broken and messy and is fermenting inside my head. Vaslav, Vaslav who is he? Everything's not alright, everything's not fine and I'm not going to sleep well for a very long time.

Miss Ann Thrope's column of Sydney smut

Miss Snitch-I'm a bitch has been down on all fours and had her ear to the ground puntresses, and no, I'm not on my knees to suck cock this time sluts. Well it's a jungle out there at the moment and not a very happy one since Martin Usher died. He was a hunk alright but never did this Miss have the exquisite pleasure of doing a pas de *dirt with him. Not like sonny boy, the terror of the Toolshed and the Queen of King's, not even a taxi to Kensington for that one but we must forgive the urgency of youth. In fact he's a bit of a dish himself and a touch more trashy than his Pa. He likes to party just like Dad, perhaps me luck'll change with baby-boy. Usher in the second generation!*

Well goss' is that maybe it wasn't suicide like they said. Maybe he was 'done in'. (Please don't cut this Mr Editor, I'm a poor piece o' filth trying to eke out a living in this festering town and any publicity is better than no publicity. I'll battle it out in the courts for the rag – promise!) Well nasties in the pris' comes as no surprise to Miss who's had a vis' herself, and what a sore girl she was après-pris'. 'Know thy enemy' brothers and sisters, it's still out there and I wouldn't be at all surprised if we've got a bit of an aboriginal-death-in-custody if you know what I mean Luvvies.

Messy biz the Usher one and hard to imagine the town without him but he'll be another candle at the vigil for Miss Ann Thrope. He was the one who signed the cheque for the halfway house for girls like myself who arrive from the cuntry with nowt but their arses to pedal. If I were a Sister of Perpetual Indulgence I'd be thinking about a canonisation for Mr Usher.

Oh and sit tight you loose-boxed slags, six more ep's of Ab Fab are on their way next year, let's hope they don't overlap with Melrose. I hear that cunt Kimberley's got something very nasty up her snatch for next week. I love me Tuesdays, they're a bitch just like me. Kiss Kiss, you're all vile but I love ya's.

CITY RHYTHM   18/11/94

My phone has gone berserk this week and I have a silent number. People I haven't spoken to in ages are ringing and leaving messages. Sherry Brown from Q.U.I.M. has been talking to both Brigitte and me. Shamash's death has raised the stakes on everything. She says *Who* have offered 25,000 dollars, and she thinks we can hold out for 32,500. Sherry seems to be sympathetic, asking me will I be up to it. How would I know?

'It's going to mean photos Hon, and probably a whole afternoon of talking. It'll be heavy shit but if you sell them an exclusive now you can still write your book when everything has died down. They want to use that photo of you giving the photographers the finger on the cover – you know, the one that won that AJA award.' I said no, if they want a photo it has to be a recent one. I hate that photo; I never want to see it again.

I went to the doctor to get more sleeping pills. There was a woman in there drinking a cask of moselle. Her face was crimson, contorted from years of drinking. I've seen her on Oxford Street many times. I used to even say hi to her but she's gotten so bad these days I don't think she passes the time with anyone anymore. She was just sitting there moaning. Occasionally she'd say, 'I just want me Pethidine or some Panedeine Forte.' Suddenly Oprah came on the TV and she was entranced, hypnotised. There was Oprah on three monitors along the wall; this woman walked up to the TV as if it were really Oprah in the flesh. 'It's me, Oprah. I come in to see ya, Love. You black like me.'

She was rocking back and forth just at the sight of her, as if Oprah were a lullaby to the destitute, a modern Messiah. She spilt a bit of her drink and the receptionist said, 'Shirl you'll have to sit down and behave yourself if you want to watch TV.' This seemed to set her off, interrupting her audience with the omnipotent. She looked back to where she had been sitting and saw an Asian girl in the next chair. She started yelling, delivering a sermon of damnation to everyone in the room.

'I tell you who gets all the money in this country, filthy fuckin' Asian slags. My people get nuthin', it's you cunts, you dirty bitches get everything.'

The receptionist was getting distressed but managed to say, 'Shirl I think it's time to go.'

The receptionist is a Greek girl, even at Shirl's level of inebriation she could ascertain that much. 'Filthy, ugly Greek whore, ugly fuckin' dago scum all of yous, ugliest fuckers in the world . . .'

She was turning, revolving as she ranted, in a rapture of abuse.

The receptionist was at a loss about what to do, not one of the waiting patients was going to say a thing. Shirl was exulted, oblivious to the urine that darkened her tracksuit pants. She was heading towards the closed doors of the doctor's rooms.

'I come for me Pethidine. I just come for me script, you bloody doctors got jobs, I know where all the money in this country goes, to you cunts . . .'

All the doctors were gradually coming out of their rooms, patiently telling her it was time to go. Everyone in the room was pretending to read magazines, safe sex brochures, even their own Medicare cards in order not to look at her. Everyone was ashamed and I could hardly stop myself from crying. I'd been so scared to go out anyway, and then this!

I had to leave; I couldn't even bear waiting to see the doctor so I'd have to just take Brigitte's valerian tablets which is something akin to taking an aspirin for a brain tumour. I was sure I was in hell, which only made me wonder what horrors had befallen that Aboriginal woman. For a moment, in the midst of her tirade, I almost felt a part of it. I imagined dancing with her as we showered the waiting room with tears, urine, racial abuse and cask wine. I realised she, like me, really only hated one person. Herself. It seemed

211

there was no God but Oprah, no refuge but the bottle or the script and heaven was merely phosphorus luminations, trapped beyond the glass of the television screen.

I spoke to Owen today. 'Oh, man, this is serious shit your ol' man dying – fucking heavy nightmare shit. Hey Vas I'm really sorry about what I said back then, you know, about you being fucked in the head from all that stuff. I never meant that dude, you know what I'm saying?'

I almost laughed for the first time since fuck knows when. Today was turning into a carnival of irony and horror.

'Owen,' I said, 'you were right when you said it. I do have serious shit in my head – my head is exploding from all the serious shit that's packed in there.'

'Hey Vas, you're not going to check out are you, like after that Newtown business?'

'Check out?'

'You know man, Kurt Cobain style, better to burn out man not fuck out.'

'Owen, I don't know what I'm gonna do, one minute I want to kill myself the next minute I'm thinking about the 30K I might get for the story. If I can get that much I'll just piss off out of Australia.'

'Just don't do anything stupid.'

'Owen, we've always done stupid things, we've chosen the most stupid and irresponsible paths since we were kids. I, like you, have consistently had no control over doing stupid things – that's why we're friends isn't it?'

He laughed this sort of Beavis and Butthead laugh. 'Oh yeah, I forgot. Hey I saw Estelle and *Marie Claire* yesterday, I told 'em where the church was for the funeral.'

'Fuck, you didn't.'

'I thought those chicks were your friends.'

'"Those chicks" have been talking to every journo in town who'll listen to them – they don't even know anything, all they want is publicity for that cunt lips show of theirs.'

'They seemed really concerned.'

'Owen, they've been on *Artributes* but they haven't even phoned me yet. Unless they're the ones that kicked in my door and left a human turd on the front steps – a choice fucking gift for the bereaved that was.'

'Did someone do that?'

'Yes, that's why I'm at Brigitte's, because I'm scared.'

'Who'd do that?'

'I don't know. It's probably nothing to do with Shamash, just some Darlo dickheads, but right now I feel really vulnerable.'

The funeral lies in wait for us and I worry about how I'll cope at that. I hope the press haven't found out where it is. David and Rosie have invited only a hundred people but many of them will go back to David's house and I know it is staked out. They haven't got their picture of Vaslav the vampire yet, they don't have the society-family-in-mourning photos and the mags are offering big bucks for some glossies. 'Sydney's Scandalous Socialite Suicide' – I can see it already. They'll print anything if I don't give them something soon.

I sat with Brigitte in her lounge room while she played this really mellow Celtic music. She was saying you've got to find somewhere inside yourself that's peaceful. She was lighting candles and burning oils – busy doing what seemed like some ceremonious ritual. Lavinia and Trismegistus (the cats) were rubbing themselves all over me, poking their bums in my face. For a moment I felt like I was under a spell and I saw Shamash as he was, I had this little movie show in my head of him pulling up in that old Volvo of his, parking about a mile out from the curb and running into the Paddo house with arms full of shopping. I saw us on the beach at some indeterminate point in our relationship, just talking. I felt him hugging me after something bad had happened at school, and just as I was doing all this Brigitte said, 'They're the things to hold onto Darl, the good things. You learn from the bad things but you hold on to the good ones.'

I got this bizarre feeling like she knew what I was thinking; it was probably just coincidence or her brilliant intuition. For a moment her whole lounge room seemed to be outside of time and space and I wasn't even stoned. The light from all those candles and lamps fused together into something ethereal; I felt the tiniest sensation of how things could be, how maybe there is a heaven or at least something better than constant bullshit.

'In a way the world isn't even real, it's imagined – a storybook,' she said.

'Yeah, Grimms' Fairytales.'

'Exactly. It's like a school full of children and like in a school, bullies often get the power but even they have their downfall because all fortunes shift. Martin was burned at the stake as surely as those thousands of witches were a few hundred years ago. We can only find the truth in the bones that are left behind Darl. A witch hunt's a witch hunt. People forget they're going to die themselves when they get a bee in their bonnets, they forget they're not already gods and forget about basic things like forgiving. What did Martin ever do to you that couldn't be forgiven by you or anyone else?'

'Nothing,' I said.

I guess it's me I'm worried about. I'm the one who really needs forgiving, and he died without letting me know if I was forgiven. I started to think about Rosie and what she would do when she found out about me not being his son. I wondered if I would still inherit but I figure if I don't get stuff as next of kin I could file a very mean palimony suit. But then I felt guilty thinking that way – money at a time like this.

FOR
SINCE
I
AM

For since I am
Love's martyr, it might breed idolatry,
If into others' hands these relics came;
As 'twas humility
To afford to it all that a soul can do,
So 'tis some bravery,
That since you would save none of me,
  I bury some of you

John Donne

It was wet and unseasonably cold for the funeral, but the weather was nothing compared to the icy sentiments that surfaced afterwards. I went in one of the mourning cars with

David and Brigitte. She was wearing a purple and gold dress (purple for freedom and gold for the spirit), and with her turban on she looked like Winnie Mandela. I wore this Frontier Aviator suit which David had bought for me. I felt extra strange wearing a suit because I never do. When we got there Owen was wearing a suit, too, one which I have never seen and one I bet he wished he never had. The trousers were too short and it was brown. The fashion victim in me recoiled but the real me was deeply touched by the effort he had made. A whole heap of Potts people were there and then a taxi turned up with Estelle and *Marie Claire*. Just as I would have expected they were in black with veils over their faces, black lipstick and hobnail boots. Estelle had a bunch of trumpet lilies and looked as though she was about to be wedded to death. *Marie Claire* made a beeline for Owen (the only person she knew) and started bitching about not being able to get a bus to this part of Mosman and how they had ended up at the zoo where they had to use some 'breeder's' mobile phone to get a taxi.

'You should have seen him, he gathered the kids around him, he thought we were going to eat them or something. I said in my sweetest voice "Us girls are in a bit of a fix and we need to call a taxi, would you be so kind as to let us use your weeny cancer transmitter?" He said there's a public phone over there and Estelle said – deadpan – "Someone has died and we don't use public phones." That seemed to do it.' Poor Owen, you could tell he didn't want to be associated with them.

Then she came over to me and said she was really sorry,

blah blah blah, and if I needed anything she would be there. I said, 'Yeah, right if it doesn't clash with any of your TV engagements.'

'Oh that, we just overheard that interviewer talking to the lawyer. I thought they might have given a biased view or something so I said we were friends.'

I had sensed the strain between David and Rosie over the last few days; I had opted out of any involvement. David felt that Martin should have his funeral at the Community Church in Darlinghurst. Rosie went so far as to look at it and said it was like a sheltered workshop for people with AIDS: 'He can't have his funeral in a place like that.'

David tried to explain that it was what Shamash would have wanted. He had done work for the mission there and it was his community. According to David, Rosie got impatient and said, 'Where was his community when he was in trouble? I didn't see legions of queens rushing to his defence from the sheltered bloody workshops our parents' money went to run, eckies and frocks is all most of them give two hoots about and then they put up a great bloody fight when they have to have a blood test for insurance. This is a family matter now. Our parents were buried by the vicar at St Oswald's, Martin was christened there and he should be sent off from there.'

David gave in, looked heavenwards and said, 'You'll never escape the North Shore, Shamash. I tried, my Darling.' That seemed to be the start of it all. Rosie looked tired and dour at the funeral. David became increasingly camp. In his speech during the service he employed the word community a number of times; he referred often to Martin's two families, his sister, his parents and his community. There was so much tension something had to give. The vicar skimmed cautiously over the events of the last three years. It was evident by his expression how difficult his whole sermon had been to prepare in a way that appeared impartial on his behalf. David wrote a great eulogy which he read during the service. It had many of us in tears:

For Martin

It is hard to see my friend – how I knew him – in my mind's eye now.

He is still like someone perfect to me but to the world, he has been garbed in filigree layers of shame.

Those who loved him don't see those layers, don't even believe they exist. So I will undress you, Martin, as I did all those years ago and perhaps we will see, once again, your coat of many colours.

I remember you in 76, fresh-faced and firing on all cylinders. Just back from the Academy. How exotic you were, barely 20 and already a much-travelled father. How romantic it all seemed, not so very long ago.

I dream of Shadforth Street, its parties and warmth. I thought you would always be there. It seemed that concrete, that real, but like all the clouds we've pinned our hearts to, it sailed away and is lost from view. We should have cherished it more at the time, laughed more heartily and hugged more closely. We should have known when life was at its best but we dared to hope for more. We were greedy men, greedy for love and for good times. Yet without that greed we'd never have had what we did. I know we'd do it all again.

I thought you'd outlive me; selfishly I hoped you would. You see, we'd already lost half of you – we've already mourned for half of you. We've become used to missing you.

What happened to all the hope? To your generously offered smiles, to your charity – which did begin at home, to your voice on the answering machine and your fingers that would firmly hold the backs of our necks as you planted kisses on us, kisses that felt like they would grow into exotic fruits.

How is it that you came to be so loathed, so attacked by people who never knew you? Why is it that those you were most supposed to have harmed would never have wished you any ill? They never left you, even as the papers tired of you, as the world left you locked away in the too-hard basket. We created a special sad kingdom in our minds, a place in which to try and share some of your horror, carry some of the blame. Perhaps the greatest pain is knowing we were ultimately unable to do that.

We are at sea Shamash, and no one's at the helm. You have carried us, loved us, bedazzled us and we shall doubt-lessly sail this ship of fools until we pass over the edge of this flat world. We'll meet you there under the crashing waters of eternity. Perhaps then we will find a kinder justice, a higher mind and a joyous freedom. I am keen to join you if this be the case.

The vicar, to David's surprise, allowed him to play Earth Wind and Fire's 'Fantasy' after the eulogy was read. David had tears running down his face as it played and so did I. It was one of Martin's favourites. He would play it at home from time to time, always trying to reach the high notes at the end. He never could and it was a joke in our place. Both David and I sang, or tried to. A couple of his musical friends joined in as well, wailing the last few bars from the song. I guess it was embarrassing but it just sort of happened. I'm not usually one to sing in public.

Things turned nasty afterwards. Rosie was very distressed. She had no family at all now except her husband. She was having some sort of grief-stricken altercation with David which I couldn't hear, then she came over to where I was standing with Brigitte. I was tensing up but made the effort to say, 'Hi Rosie'. She wasn't coming to pay respects, however. She pulled me away looking very distressed.

'Vaslav, I don't know I'll be able to see you again. Since you came into our family we've had nothing but pain and tragedy. I don't know what you're to blame for and at the moment I don't care, but what I'm left with doesn't feel like a family anymore and if family is such an ill-fated affair I'd do better without it.'

I was speechless. Thel must have heard because she came over. 'Rosie don't, Love. You're very upset and they're not fair things to be saying right now. There are a good many things you don't know my girl, many of which you'll need to keep in touch with Vas to find out. It would break Martin's heart to hear this sort of thing – break his heart, do you hear!' Thel was starting to cry, fishing in her handbag for a tissue. Rosie wandered off in a daze towards her husband.

Brigitte came over and closed her arms around me. We both looked at each other. 'You'll have to forgive that one, Darl. You're both very sad souls right now.' I sniffled and said, 'We never liked each other that much, I never see her anyway – don't want to either.' David looked over and saw tears on my face. He, too, had sensed what Rosie had said. He held up my face in his hands and kissed it. 'Don't listen to her, Vas. She's out of her head, and she is not Shamash. I think deep down she resents him for having been so well loved. Rosie has always tried so hard and Martin did it effortlessly. She doesn't know what she's saying at the moment.'

Rosie left with her husband, even though David tried to get them to his place. It seemed as if she had turned her back on her brother's life. Thelly and Dianne came over. 'You've still got us as family, Vaslav, I want you to know that. You can come and stay with me in Homebush whenever you want.' Thel put her arms around me. 'I'm going to move up to Katoomba soon. Di and I have been looking at houses and we think our offer on one will be accepted. I don't want to live near that Olympic Village when it comes. I'll be too old for all that nonsense. You could come up there to escape Darlinghurst, would you like that?'

'Yes Thelly, I'd like that.'

'I remember how you used to love going up there on that scenic railway, how you would nag your father to take you up there after that time you, Dianne and I had gone. You two loved it but I have no stomach for heights. Martin used to say he never got a moment's peace after that trip. You know I think he might have burned himself out even sooner if he hadn't had you there. It's true Vas, before he brought you back he was far too wild, you calmed him down and made him grow up a lot. You gave him all the respectability he felt he would never have been able to have. His family never really accepted his lifestyle you know. You see, I know more about him and you than you might think. I saw your first passport and I asked Martin a few things, I believe you saved him from a life of melancholy and destructiveness. It's important you see it that way too, Pet. Remember, you're the boy who didn't drown in that crash – so don't drown now.' She winked and I wondered how much Shamash had told her. I would ask her one day soon. She stroked my hair, Dianne gave me a kiss and off they went into the grey North Shore yonder.

The rain began to bucket down, and everything seemed drab. People still stood around with running mascara until finally we headed off to David's. There was no crematorium service and only about thirty people came back. I managed to get rid of Essie and Macca, leaving them gossiping at the bus stop as we cut through the rain in our 'pearl' coloured mourning limo. Estelle had kept one of the trumpet lilies and was rhythmically slapping *Marie Claire*'s face with it. It was annoying her, I could tell. She tore it out of Estelle's hand and threw it into the bushes. As they faded from view I could just see Macca mouthing 'fuck off' to Estelle.

I hid under Shamash's big black coat. I could still smell him in it, I'm sure I could. As we dashed from the car the few photos that were taken would not have shown my face. Inside I began to cheer up for a moment. I almost smiled.

Those cunts weren't going to get another blotchy-faced photo of me. We all got drunk on martinis, not a favourite of mine but quick to work. There seemed to be no other drinks except for Thelly's sherry. David says the one party we'd all like most to attend is our wake. I think what Thel said helped me and so did the drinks.

In the end I asked Owen to come and stay at my place. He was drinking sherry too because the martinis tasted like snake poison to him. I couldn't help taking the piss out of him, Owen, the poo-brown-suited sherry sipper.

'I'll find you something else to wear at my dive.'

'What's wrong with this?'

'A shit-coloured suit that might have fitted you ten years ago? Nothing.'

'You're a cunt, Usher.'

'You're an arsehole, Henley.'

'Glove puppet Usher.'

'Turd-faced Henley.'

We wandered back through Elizabeth Bay, the grown-ups worrying about us. David says I take after my father: 'Three martinis and he's king of the world.'

When we got down the road Owen said, 'Hey dude, you're gunna be rich aren't you?'

'I guess.'

'What'll you do?'

'I dunno, piss off.'

I kicked an empty beer bottle into a waiting styrofoam McDonald's burger box. 'Goal,' I screamed as it hit the wall and splintered into dangerous fragments.

Owen said, 'You need a syringe on either side for points.'

I gave him a dark look. 'You mean for penalties.'

I looked around at all the neon and drizzle; it was like *Blade Runner*. 'That's what I like about inner Sydney. It's a stinking cesspit where no one gives a fuck – there is a constant amnesty on environmentalism and morality here. Shoot, shit and shag where you like. If you don't like this life Owen, you can always get another one. That's what Shamash has done, pissed this joint off. I can feel that he's okay sometimes. Does that sound weird?'

'Yeah, it's weird but I can dig it, he was alright your ol' man.'

'Yeah, I reckon he was alright.'

S P E N D

When my story was printed in the November issue of *ismag* it was their biggest selling edition yet. In the end they offered something like the 30K Q.U.I.M. had been negotiating. Telling the story really was a catharsis for me in a way. The interviewer suspected I was lying; I had to spend two hours going over my abduction in all its detail before she could move on to other things. We did a photo shoot on Brigitte's back balcony – they used one of a sad, ponderous me looking towards Centrepoint as well as some growing-up ones I gave them. According to *ismag*, 'Only the most unscrupulous and immoral of men would eavesdrop on the quiet murmurings of Vaslav's dawning sexuality, seeking to take that which was not yet on offer . . .'

Rosie has been a bit more civil with me since the funeral, allowing me to use a picture of her and me in the article. She was in shock of course, but said she never quite believed

I was Shamash's son. I took that to be a genuine insult but said nothing more about it. Decency got the better of me. I will try to get on with her for Shamash's sake.

The will was easy. I was left the house and a bit of money. Perhaps now that woman who told me I was weird for hanging around and staring at the house might treat me with some respect since I'm her landlord. Everything left for me in the will was left specifically to me. It didn't matter whether I was Shamash's son or not. I sensed that Rosie saw my inheritance as an appalling misplacement of possessions, that I'm somehow not worthy of establishment wealth, but tough for Cosy North Shore Rosie.

No way could I have stayed in Sydney, not with all that publicity at work. I fucked off straight after Christmas and left all the legal matters in David's hands. I'm still abandoning responsibility. Here in Paris I'm enjoying getting tanked up at night on cocaine and Scotch. Warming myself up enough with whisky to face the freezing night outside; coked up enough to negotiate my way socially with the new 'friends' I've met. They're mostly like me – the wrong crowd, transients, Eurotrash, daytime neurotics, night-time in-crowd.

I bought Owen a ticket to come stay with me for a month; I wanted to be with someone I knew for a while. He'll get a real blast living like a king for a spell. I know I should try to save some money but now I have the rent from the house which is $750 a week. David says I should make sure I keep an account for repairs and rates and shit: 'They will be your responsibility now.' Yeah, yeah, I said. A dangerous young man like myself can manage quite well on that much;

besides I'm still living on the magazine money. I bought Brigitte a new computer and she's written to me on it twice already.

I know my way around another little ghetto now, only here I have no past, no scandal. Here I don't mean anything. Here, as long as I pay my hotel bill, as long as *je suis discret* they tolerate me. My money vanishes at an alarming rate; over counters, up my nose and down my throat. At last I feel free to be the slut I was perhaps destined to be. My friend Michel (another gay remittance boy from some province or region I'm unlikely to visit) says '*Mais non, un slut cheri, un courtisane, oui?*'

'*Non, un* fucking slut.' The French of course don't understand my vulgarity. They don't have to – I won't be troubling them with it for too long.

I told David I'd come back and work at the theatre in April; we both know that I am still good for business even if it's just so people can gawk at me. The trouble is I get nervous, and you can't have coke all the time to give you confidence; we all know where that ends.

I don't seem to really enjoy sex now unless I'm loaded to some extent, but I still have it just the same, more even. I dare say I'll become one of those hard-bitten old queens if I live long enough; even that's in the lap of the gods.

Brigitte said in her first letter, 'I hate to think what you're getting up to over there.' I answered her with, Why don't you come see for yourself Honey Bun? It's just *partie partie partie in Gai Paris pour moi.*

'You just take it easy,' she said in the second. I'm writing to her now to say, 'I do Brigitte, I do.'

She sent me more books – one's called *Manholes to Heaven: Trapdoors to Hell*. I sent her a photo of the catacombs and said, I've already been through the trapdoor. I think she's probably got a different interpretation of what manholes to heaven might mean, and I'm sure she'd find that mine is far too literal.

I have fulfilled one ambition here. I got myself in a porn movie. It wasn't one of Jean Daniel Cadinot's, sadly. He is my favourite pornographer in the whole world. Nor was it as squalid as I'd hoped it might be. My appearance was only a cameo (by cameo I mean I was only fucked once by Bruno Luc, the hero of this *particulaire* tale). I've not seen the finished product but I thought it would be a good addition to my collection of vices. I even thought it could be shrink-wrapped with my book one day – a sort of cross-merchandising Father's Day gift idea. I figure when I get old it'll be good to show the grandkids. Someone else's.

For the film I had to catch a train out to this big old stately home. I was supposed to be a servant boy, and my dialogue was kept to an absolute minimum because my French is so bad. I wore a little bellhop outfit (for a minute), and when they'd done with me they gave me 2000 francs, a vodka and tonic, a line of coke and a limo back into Paris. It wasn't a huge amount of money but at least the film looked classy by porn standards. Also, I stole the bellhop jacket, which looks really cute with my Jean-Paul Gaultier trousers. One thing most people probably don't realise about porn is that some of those camera angles you get require a lot of intrusive manoeuvring. Now I know how women feel when they have to go to a gynaecologist. The French, despite their Catholicism and conservatism, treat sex in a very exciting and matter-of-fact way. It's all about how masculine you are, how strong, how much you can endure.

If I want to live dangerously that is my business. Whatever has happened to me in my 21 years has left me a stranger to safety. Given the choice of a look around Quay-West sauna or Notre Dame Cathedral I think you know where I'd most likely be found. Sure I miss Brigitte, Thel and David, but I also think they heaved a sigh of relief when I took off. They know I've either got to look after myself or not. It's not up to them anymore, and why should it be? They've all done their best with this prodigal varmint. I still wish I'd seen Shamash again. I wish he'd written, even a suicide note, though God knows what the story is there – that could take months to resolve.

I send the folks back home pictures of me drinking Scotch on top of Jim Morrison's grave, smoking a cigarette on Oscar Wilde's fantastic deco death ship, pictures of *me avec une grande baguette* (why a baguette would be feminine I don't know). The monster is loose, making his porn, behaving like trash with all the other dangerous young men, then coming back to the comforts of an expensive hotel. I'm not blaming anyone anymore. I take responsibility for myself, living like I do. That takes a lot of courage. I'm on the edge, sure, but I've got to try to have a good time in the ways I know how. Even Brigitte says debauchery and asceticism can be means to the same end. She just has a clearer idea of that end than I do.

I hope, on my return, I'll be stable enough to pull it off – the job, the wealth, the book even. People will be waiting to see me fall just like they watched Shamash. The world is a butcher's shop and we're all meat for the chopping.

Last night at Quay-West I crossed all the safety barriers. I met this German guy who spoke a little French and no English, but it didn't matter because it wasn't the sort of meeting that required dialogue. He looked dangerous and beautiful, but he turned out to be more dangerous than anything else. I was coked, and even though I felt horny I couldn't get a decent erection. He could and was single-minded about wanting to fuck me. We were in a cubicle; he had no intention of using a condom. I got this beautiful body rush from the cocaine, and for a moment I wasn't concerned about condoms. I relaxed, totally, as he hammered into me. I felt as though it was someone else down there being fucked. I was in a trance and each thrust seemed to dislodge a memory as if I were undergoing a kind of cerebral colonic irrigation:

In he'd go.

I'd see the swings and slides at the council estate.

Out he'd come.

Once more I'd see the shadowy face of the man in the black anorak, the 20 pence glinting in the pale sunlight.

In he'd go.

I'd see my Mum caught in the dog-like motions of shagging, her face fixed on the ceiling.

Out.

Shamash, totally giving in to me, being there with me and

for me, a distantly remembered fuck that meant something.

In.

The scenic railway with Shamash, and ice-creams.

Out.

Shamash, grey, dead, not the same person, and that bottle of hair conditioner.

In.

Platform shoes and pusher, neighbours shouting at each other on the council estate.

I looked up at this dude, who was not particularly interested in me beyond that slick, fleshy tunnel he was ploughing with hearty primal devotion. 'Listen, you Kraut bastard,' I said, 'you're going to cum inside me and you couldn't give a shit. You'll cum, wipe yourself on a towel and vanish under the cloud of shame that will descend as soon as you feel *le petit mort.*' He didn't understand a word of what I said, and I don't know whether it was a fleeting moment of self-preservation or a shift in my mood from the cocaine. Whatever it was, I pushed him off me and left him like a shag on a rock. You see, I realised something – I realised as much as I would like to, it is not possible to live life as pornography. I love pornography but ultimately it doesn't work. It lacks an enduring philosophy and my life seems based or debased on its central tenet; an ephemeral ejaculation and its ensuing void.

I would have liked, on one level, to have abandoned myself to him, to not have cared, but I couldn't. I'm sure to many people the whole scenario would be considered appalling, but to me it was an affirmation of worth. It was sad because it was the death of a belief system but a relief to realise I still had limits. To me it was a breakthrough. I know the safe-sex brigade would say I'd still taken a shocking risk, but I'm not concerned about that. For me sex has always been as much about death as it has about life, intrinsic to both, preprogrammed, and my programming exists at one end of a preordained polarity with boring pristine celibacy lurking at the other.

Sure, I went and had sex with someone else after that, but it was safer and the images changed too. With the next person I seemed to descend into my subconscious, remembering the dream of the car crash. It was weird – I was being fucked while almost falling asleep. Then, from inside this half sleep, I realised we weren't even in the front of the car, we were both in the back, Shamash and I; it was a taxi and neither of us was driving. I don't know who the driver was or where he was taking us but I'm going to call that driver fate. I don't want to see his face and I don't want to pay his fare.

I'll be home soon – March, April, whenever. Those media people can sharpen their cleavers; Fred Nile can sharpen his wits. I'll get waxed, tanned and detoxed on the way back. I'll be ready. Perhaps I can launch the book and the vid together; it's called *Devinette Devant* (even porn sounds classy in French). Let the French test their filthy bombs – there's something comforting about toxic waste, something funny about how in spite of all the rhetoric in the world no country with any international clout will really lift a finger to save the world we pretend we love. If the law's an ass then morality is a lumberjack. It's all a joke really, and I think Brigitte's right – it's an imagined playground full of bullies, victims and all the inbetweenies. No one grows up; they just fancy they do. Victims turn into bullies or vice versa and all the practice you ever needed was a game of musical chairs as a kid. More and more I hope the world's not real. I'm starting to count on it.

Brigitte says the minute you start counting on it, the less real it will become. 'It'll frighten you, hurt you and thrill you some more but in the end it'll bore you and you'll be looking inside your head for the challenges you need. That's the way it should be. The apple's got a core Darl, and when you've devoured the flesh the seeds still remain. They don't look nearly as tasty but they are where the future lies. Bury them in the ground when you've had enough of eating the flesh and thousands more will grow. The great lie and the worst fear most people have is that somewhere along the way they might have sold their soul. The truth is Darl, that's the part we never owned to begin with.'

When Brigitte writes me all this stuff I think yeah, yeah, but sometimes it's like, with all the blood, guts, needles and buses I go on about or all the trashy DF sex I do, I sense there is something that never gets touched. Something no amount of hammering can knock out. When I feel that way, I get this idea that it's alright to play my shocking part. That this is the only dimension where debauchery is up for exploration. So I explore.

'Bring me another boy, this one is full!'

EPILOGUE

I sit in a bar near Rue St Martin, huddled within the folds of Shamash's big black coat. My chest is sore because I've just had a tattoo carved into it – the same one my Mum used to have. I saw it in the window of a tattoo salon on the Rue de Clichy and took it as an omen.

I've walked past the hotel where I stayed all those years ago with Shamash and Ashley. Now I'm drinking Scotch and coke as well as hot coffee to warm my hands. In my pocket is a cheese pastry thing I bought on the street. I keep taking big greasy chunks off it, and now it's nearly gone. I'm sure this would be considered gauche in here. The Johnny part of me likes to be common, likes to behave like a dero; the Vas part of me indulges him in that. I can smell my own body odour because despite the cold, I was sweating with pain while the tat was being done. Snow has been falling for the first time since I've been here, and I feel good in one of my favourite Vaslavian ways. Owen will be here tomorrow, and that will be excellent.

Two men nearby are talking intimately in that cool, sexy way French people have. I've come to love it since I've been here, though, like everything in Paris, I'll always be ultimately excluded from it. My eyes dart over to them, and I realise they are talking about me. I get that cruise shiver, the feeling of excitement you get when you realise you're being included in something and bypassed at the same time. It's like not knowing whether you might be asked out for dinner or whether you will be dinner. Not speaking much French and not being of any public interest in this part of the world, I wouldn't be so naive as to suppose they were considering me for an enduring friendship or an intellectual discussion. They whisper again while I stuff the last piece of pastry into my mouth. You don't really need to be French to know what they're saying. The spirit of some things speaks for itself:

'*Tu vois ce mec, qu'est-ce que tu crois qu'il serait capable de faire?*'

'*Le mec – là ferait n'importe quoi!*'

Is it that obvious? I ask myself, feeling self-conscious again. I look down at my coffee and feel flakes of the pastry blighting my lips. I drink the last of the Scotch, trying to sink further into the coat as colour rises to my cheeks. It's damp near my tat – it must be bleeding a little. Suddenly, I'm lonely and a little sad, but overall, I think I'm doing fine.

NEAL DRINNAN was born in 1964 in Melbourne, Australia, and was dubiously educated at various (now defunct) high schools and Camberwell Boys' Grammar. At the age of seventeen, he abandoned his education and suburban family home life for the lure of Chapel Street and life's more ephemeral things. He has worked in publishing for many years, has been a frequent contributor to *OUTRAGE* magazine, and is a regular columnist for Sydney's *Capital Q*. He lives in South Wales, Australia. *Glove Puppet* is his first novel.